POWER OF MAGIC

LINSEY HALL

1

The alarm blared, a shrieking warning of oncoming disaster.

I surged upright before my eyes were even open, instinct propelling me toward wakefulness.

"What is it?" Maximus's groggy voice sounded from beside me in the bed.

"Attack. The castle is under attack." I scrambled out of bed, throwing the blanket aside and hitting the ground running. I raced around the room, searching for the clothes I'd discarded in haste the night before. Where were my damned pants? I needed pants.

A quick glance at the clock showed that it was three a.m., which was definitely not a pants hour. Unless you were about to defend a castle. Doing that in my underwear was a bad plan.

Maximus was out of bed in an instant, his strong body totally naked. Under any other circumstance, I'd have paused to admire him. But not now. Right now, I needed to get to the castle walls.

Were the Titans attacking? We'd fought them only five days ago, binding their dark magic so it couldn't spread through the world anymore. They'd disappeared and we hadn't heard from them since—nor had we managed to locate them—but they had to be pissed at us.

Finally, I located my last pair of clean underwear and tugged on some old jeans that had seen better days. A bra and shirt came next, followed by my leather jacket. As I tugged them on, a sharp pain twinged in my side.

I pressed a hand to the spot. "Ouch."

"What is it?" Maximus asked as he tugged a shirt over his head.

"Nothing. Just a weird stitch I've been feeling in my side lately."

"How lately?"

"Just a few days. It's already faded."

Maximus frowned at me. "A few days?"

"Yeah, so?"

"We were with the Titans five days ago. Could it be related to that?"

"I don't know." I hated that idea so much that I shoved it to the back of my mind. "Come on. We need to go."

He gave me a look that said he wouldn't be forgetting this, and we exited the bedroom in a rush, racing down the spiral stairs to the living room.

The Menacing Menagerie sat on the couch, their eyes wide. They'd been banished to sleeping on the couch once Maximus and I had taken our relationship to the next level, which we'd done immediately after our run-in with the Titans five days ago.

What's going on? Romeo's bright eyes met mine.

"We're under attack."

Eloise perked up, her little badger face clearly excited. The light of battle gleamed in her eyes, and she grinned, her teeth sharp and fierce. Poppy smiled, too, the little possum nudging her badger friend.

"Well, come on, then," I said as I grabbed my potion belt off the kitchen counter and strapped it around my waist. My potion bag came next, and I shoved as many bombs as I could gather into the leather bag.

I might be mastering my Dragon God magic, but I didn't ever think I'd give up my potions.

The five of us hurried from the apartment, spilling out into the darkened hallway. The door slightly down the way opened, and Bree and Cade rushed out. The Pugs of Destruction were already racing down the hall, their ghostly blue forms bright in the darkness.

"What's happening?" Bree demanded, her dark hair messy and her T-shirt on backward.

"No idea." I joined her in a sprint down the hall.

As we passed Ana's door, it opened. The Cats of Catastrophe streaked out, three blurs of black, orange, and white. Ana and Lachlan followed them out the door.

"Know what's going on?" Ana asked, her voice breathless. Her blonde hair was piled in a messy knot.

"Nope," Bree and I said in unison.

Together, the six of us sprinted down the hall, our animal familiars racing along like a tiny four-legged army of weirdness. The sound of doors slamming and shouts echoed through the hall as the rest of the Protectorate headed toward the castle walls.

We sprinted into the entrance, a massive room at the front of the castle. Hans, the cook, appeared at the top of the stairs that led down to the kitchen, his eyes wide and a big wooden spoon gripped in his hand. Boris the rat, his constant companion, rode on his head, clinging to his perch on top of the chef's hat. Florian, the ghostly night librarian, appeared a moment later, along with Lavender and Angus, my fellow classmates.

By the time we ran out the front door and into the courtyard, there were nearly two dozen of us, all dragged from our beds.

We raced across the lawn, the moonlight illuminating the dark grass.

Near the main castle gate, I spotted Jude standing on top of the castle wall. We veered for her, sprinting as a group. Stairs led up to the ramparts at a dozen strategic points along the castle wall. I raced up the nearest set, my lungs burning.

The sight that greeted me on the other side of the wall dropped my heart into my stomach.

"Holy fates." I leaned on the castle wall, scanning the crowd that stood below.

There were hundreds of Magica and demons, armed to the teeth. Magic sparked around the lot of them, dark and fierce. It made my skin itch and my hackles rise. They weren't attacking —not yet—but they were ready to.

The demons looked normal—that is to say, like a bunch of evil jerks. But the Magica...

"There's a manic glow in their eyes," Ana murmured.

"Like they're entranced," Bree said.

I nodded, my heart thundering. "They're under the Titans' thrall. They have to be."

We knew that the Titans' dark magic was converting humans into cult worshippers who were filled with dark magic, but seeing them was a whole different thing.

There were so many.

"They look like the worshippers we met back at the Titans' island fortress." Maximus gripped my hand. "But how did they get here?"

I scanned the forest behind the army, but spotted no portal gleaming in the distance.

Jude strode up to us, her face set in stern lines and her starry blue eyes shadowed with exhaustion. We'd been searching for the Titans for five days, and that was on top of the exhausting search that had happened before. No one looked good now, especially not our leader.

"They snuck up during the night," Jude said. "Silent and swift. We only noticed they were there when Hedy went for a walk on the walls because she couldn't sleep."

"Why aren't they attacking?" Maximus asked.

"They can't," Jude said. "At least, not yet. There are a lot of them, but they're no match for the protection charms on the castle walls."

The castle had been attacked earlier that year. As a result, the Protectorate had reinforced our boundaries.

"How much more magic would they need to break through?" Maximus asked.

Jude turned toward the army, a frown creasing her brow. "I don't know. More. Which they could probably get."

"If the Titans joined them, they might be able to get past our defenses?" I asked.

She pursed her lips. "Probably."

"So let's launch the first attack," Bree said. "Take them out before they can do damage."

Jude shook her head and pointed. "There are too many. And see the shimmer in the air? They've got some kind of protection spell on them. I don't know what it would take to get through there, but I'd want a bigger army on our side before we tried."

Maximus propped his hands on the waist-high castle wall and stared at the army. "I think they are a warning of some kind. If they were going to attack, they already would have."

"A warning of what, though?" Cade asked.

"No idea."

The rest of us murmured our agreement. If they were going to attack, they wouldn't just be standing here, giving us warning to beef up our defenses.

Jude cupped her hands around her mouth and shouted, "What do you want?"

The army was silent for a moment, then a figure stepped forward and shouted, his voice loud and clear, "Rowan Blackwood."

Well, shit.

My heart thudded hard against my ribs, and Maximus's hand tightened on mine.

"Well, they can't have you," Bree muttered.

"Not happening," Jude shouted. She turned her back on him and opened her mouth to speak.

Before she could say a word, a voice echoed from the comms charm around my throat. "Rowan? It's Queen Penthesilea. We need you at headquarters. The Great One wants to speak to you."

My gaze darted to Jude. I was loyal to the Amazons, but the Protectorate came first. And since we were currently under attack because of me....

"Go," Jude said. "They clearly aren't going to attack now, and even if they did, it would take them days to get through our defenses with their numbers. See what this *Great One* has to say."

"Who *is* the Great One?" Bree asked.

"She's like their wise woman. An oracle of sorts. The queens have consulted her on my behalf before, but she's never wanted to speak to me directly."

"It can't be a coincidence." Jude waved her hand at the army that waited outside the gates. "No way they show up at the same time the mysterious Great One wants to see you."

"I'll go. But call me immediately if you need me," I said.

"We'll figure out what the hell is going on here," Jude said. "In the meantime, see what you can learn. This could be what leads us to the Titans."

I nodded, sharing one last glance with my sisters, then looked at Maximus. "Do you have a transport charm I can use?"

He nodded and dug into his pocket, then handed two over. "I'm going to visit the Order headquarters and see if they've learned anything new, but be careful with the Great One."

"I'm sure she's fine."

"Maybe." He pulled me close and kissed my forehead.

I blushed, since we were standing right in front of everyone, but I couldn't help but smile.

I turned from him, leaned over the castle railing, and shouted, "I'm leaving, so there's no point in attacking."

Jude grinned. "Nice touch."

"I thought so." I made sure to stand near the wall when I chucked the transport charm to the ground. I wanted the army to see me disappear. A silver cloud exploded upward. Right before stepping in, I caught Jude's gaze. "Seriously, call me if you need me."

She nodded, and it was the last thing I saw before the ether sucked me in and spun me through space.

I arrived in the main lobby of the Amazons' headquarters in Istanbul a few minutes later. The street outside of their building had been quiet. Since it was essentially the business district, it didn't stay alive with nightlife like other parts of town.

Which was for the best, since the Menacing Menagerie accompanied me for the first time ever. A raccoon, a possum, and a badger would be pretty out of place in Istanbul's most professional neighborhood. I pushed open the big glass door that led into the lobby of the Amazons' headquarters. Two guards stood in the middle, their keen eyes traveling over us.

The Menagerie's little toenails clicked on the marble floor of the lobby as we walked toward them.

They rose to their feet as we neared. Their black tactical gear was neat and pressed as usual, and they stood at perfect attention.

"The queens are waiting for you on the bottom level," said the one on the right. Her dark hair gleamed in a long tail down her back, and she shared a look with the blonde at her side. Her expression was serious and slightly worried. It had to be about whatever I would find in the basement. I shifted uncomfortably.

The Great One was always spoken about in hushed tones, and I doubted I'd be sitting at her desk and asking a few questions.

"I will escort you." She gestured toward the elevators.

"Thanks." I hurried toward the elevator bank, the warrior at my side. There was a palpable tension in the air that I didn't normally feel when I visited. The Menagerie followed, and for once, Romeo kept his mouth shut. Honestly, it made me even more nervous.

When we reached the elevator doors, the Amazon reached out and typed a code into the number panel on the right side of the door.

Magic sparked on the air, and a little light turned green on the number panel. Right beneath it, a small silver panel opened to reveal a dark nook in the wall.

"Stick your hand in there like this." She raised her hand and stuck out her index finger, then held it so her palm faced the ceiling.

I mimicked the gesture and stuck my fingertip into the little cubby. A sharp pain pricked the fleshy pad of my finger, and I winced. "Ouch."

"Just a little blood magic to make sure your intentions are pure."

I withdrew my finger and shook it. "They are."

The elevator doors zipped open.

"It seems the spell agrees." The Amazon grinned at me. "Good luck."

"Thanks." I shot her a wary look as I stepped inside.

The Menagerie followed, apparently immune to the need for testing.

As the elevator zoomed to the bottom floor, I wondered how everyone was doing back at the castle.

Had the army attacked yet? Once they did, would we have time to mount our defenses?

Fates, I hoped so.

The elevator descended into the ground, and every few seconds, magic popped against my skin. It felt like protection charms, and they were strong.

Did the Great One herself reside down here, or was it just her office? Was she even a person?

The elevator dinged, and the doors whooshed open.

My gaze zeroed in on the flaming portal that stood in the middle of the empty space. It flickered with red and black light, and just the sight of it made me nervous. I'd never seen a portal that looked quite so ominous, and it was the only thing in the room.

This was a sacred space, a secret space. And if I wanted to meet the Great One, I'd probably have to step through that creepy portal.

I shivered at the idea, then stiffened my spine.

"Rowan, that was quick." Queen Penthesilea's voice echoed across the large, empty room.

I looked toward her, spotting the two queens standing to the right of the portal. The black and red lights had caught my attention so fully that I hadn't noticed them at first.

As usual, both queens were dressed in the Amazons' signature black battle gear, with their hair pulled back tightly from their faces. They were tall and graceful, looking like they could take on giants if they were so inclined. Their magic filled the air around them, making it clear that these were some seriously powerful women.

"You said the Great One wanted to see me?" I walked toward them.

"She does," Queen Hippolyta said. "It is rare that she requests an audience, but we feel that she will likely impart valuable information to you."

Rare was right. I'd only ever heard whispers of her, but never spoken to an Amazon who had actually seen her, other than the queens.

"I hope she's got something big," I said. "Because shit has really hit the fan back at the Protectorate." I stopped in front of them. The Menacing Menagerie lined up behind me, clearly on their best behavior. I didn't need to look at them to know they were trying to be good. The silence made that obvious enough.

"You've brought your little army." Queen Hippolyta smiled slightly. She totally liked my tiny dumpster divers. Couldn't blame her.

"My armed guards," I said.

"Quite impressive." She smiled at them, and I glanced back, catching sight of Romeo giving her a wink. "Unfortunately, they cannot accompany you through the portal as they were not invited. And really, it's no place for animals."

I swallowed hard as I glanced at the portal, which was still majorly creeping me out.

Romeo gripped the leg of my jeans. *I'm not keen on going in there.*

"Ditching me so soon?" I asked him.

Just making sure I'm around to save your butt from the Titans.

I reached down and ruffled his little head. "Fair enough." I looked at Queens Penthesilea and Hippolyta. "Do you know why the Great One wants to speak with me now?"

"We believe something has changed recently, but we do not know what," said Queen Hippolyta.

"Well, I'd better go find out." Despite my nerves, I was desperate for answers. We'd been hunting the Titans for five days with no luck. Anything that would help me find them—and defeat them—was welcome.

"Then come on." Queen Penthesilea gestured me forward, toward the glowing red and black lights.

We walked toward the portal, and I stopped in front of it. Queen Penthesilea stood at my left, and Queen Hippolyta at my right. The Menagerie lined up behind me.

The portal flickered with black and red flames. Heat billowed out, roasting my cheeks and drying my eyes. I blinked, squinting into the eyes of death. I'd never seen a portal with eyes, but this one had two massive red irises that stared straight at me. Something deep in my soul told me that this was death. Despite the massive heat, my skin chilled.

Fates, this was creepy.

Queen Penthesilea sucked in a breath. "If you want to speak to the Great One, you must walk through the flames of the portal and face your greatest fear."

"Knowledge does not come without sacrifice, and the Great One demands that you earn your way into her audience."

I'd known this wouldn't be easy.

"My greatest fear is death?" That didn't sound quite right.

I didn't want to die, of course, but I'd never thought that was my greatest fear. If I died, I'd just be...dead. I wouldn't be around to be miserable about it.

"Look closer." Queen Penthesilea pointed at the portal.

I squinted, gasping when I spotted the pattern that flickered red and black around the eyes. "My sisters."

They were dying amongst the flames, the fire devouring their forms.

"That's not all," Queen Hippolyta said.

I blinked, looking harder. There were more people in the fire. Jude and Hedy and everyone I'd ever known. They were *all* dying. Even the Protectorate castle was going up in the inferno. So was the Amazons' headquarters.

"As far as fears go, I'd say that one is fairly common," Queen Penthesilea said.

"Losing everything and everyone I love?" I shivered.

"Yes." She tapped her chin. "Though the dentist is a popular one too. Also, a tax audit." Queen Hippolyta turned to me, her expression more serious than her voice. "Except that you have a very good reason for your fear, given your current circumstances."

"Are you ready?" Queen Penthesilea asked.

I wasn't, but it didn't matter. I *had* to be ready. Because Queen Hippolyta was right. I did have a very good reason for my fear.

The misery I was seeing within the portal could happen. It wasn't some random nightmare. With the Titans on earth, this vision could easily be the future.

Last week, I'd failed to stop the Titans. I may have succeeded in limiting their magic, but the three massively powerful Greek deities were still out there, hatching a plan that would result in the death of everything and everyone I loved.

I swallowed hard and nodded. "I can do this."

Queen Penthesilea squeezed my arm. "Good. Because you don't have a choice."

"We believe in you, though," Queen Hippolyta said.

Their confidence bolstered my confidence. I hadn't been an Amazon for long since I'd only come into my power a couple weeks ago. But in that amount of time, I'd grown to love my new sisters-in-arms. The queens were intimidating, but I respected them. Cared for them.

And they were here to help me find the answers to stopping the Titans. Even though they were telling me to step into the mega scary death-portal, I knew it was for the best.

I straightened my shoulders and stepped through the flames.

Immediately, grief stabbed me like an icicle through the heart. I gasped, doubling over. An agony of loss tore the muscles from my bones and pulverized my brain. I felt like a mass of jello, or some kind of sea slug that was glued to the bottom of the ocean by the weight of millions of tons of water.

Holy fates, this was awful.

I wasn't just confronting the *idea* of the loss of everyone I loved. I was experiencing what it would feel like.

I'd rather die.

No question.

I sucked in a ragged breath that burned my lungs. I couldn't die. I had to keep going, because if I didn't stop the Titans, this horrible future would come true.

"Keep going." Queen Penthesilea's voice echoed through the pain that nearly broke my hearing.

"You can't stop," Queen Hippolyta said. "Prove your strength."

I clung to her words as I forced my foot forward, feeling like I was walking through a swamp of pain. Visiting the Amazons' Great One was a rare honor—I had to earn it.

It took everything I had, but I forced myself to walk through the misery of the portal. Finally—*finally*—the ether caught hold of me and sucked me in, spinning me through space and delivering me to my final destination.

When I was thrust out into the bright sunlight of a summer day, I staggered, going to my knees.

Groggy, my head aching like a piano had fallen on it, I

blinked. Soft green grass sprouted up from between my finger-tips. I dug them into the earth, grounding myself.

Fates.

Memories of what I'd seen echoed through my head. Flashes of burning bodies and tortured faces. *My loved ones.*

I squeezed my eyes shut and shook my head so hard my brain rattled.

It only worked a little. There were still faded images lurking at the edges of my consciousness, but I didn't have time to focus on the misery. I needed to keep going.

Keep moving.

Keep working.

Or the Titans would win.

I surged to my feet, head spinning, and looked around.

I stood in a beautiful field full of fresh spring grass and wild flowers. The sun beat down warmly, making the flowers gleam like jewels amongst the emerald blades.

I blinked.

Well, this was different.

So...nice.

Such a contrast to the portal.

In the distance, a glowing golden light shined brightly against the grass. On instinct, I walked toward it. Magic rolled toward me, intensely powerful.

There was someone sitting within the light. I could make out the faintest outline of a person. A woman. But it was her magic that really slapped me in the face.

Holy fates, she was strong.

As I neared, the light faded until it revealed a pale golden ghost of a woman. She sat cross-legged on the grass, and her body was so transparent that I could barely make out her features when her head tilted up toward me. She looked like a modernist watercolor painting done in shades of gold.

"You are the Dragon God." Her voice echoed with power that made my muscles tremble.

"Um, yeah." I held out my arms. "Do I live up to expectations?"

"That is, as of yet, unclear."

I swallowed hard and nodded, suddenly nervous. "Fair enough."

"Sit." She gestured.

I followed her command, my insides thrumming with tension. I hoped she'd just blurt out some useful information for me—maybe all the answers to my problems. But since that sounded too good to be true, maybe she'd let me ask some questions.

I had a seemingly impossible problem, after all. It was the perfect kind of thing to ask someone called the Great One. How to stop the three most powerful magical beings in the universe?

Would she even be able to help?

"I can feel your doubt."

"Sorry." *Dang it, keep it together.* "It's just that I've got a really big problem."

"They all do."

I nodded. "Well, this is the biggest problem for right now." It was an understatement, actually. "And I think it's the reason you called me to you."

"Indeed, it is." The shadowy golden figure stretched out her arm and turned her palm upward. "Give me your hand."

I didn't hesitate. This was way easier than talking. I stuck my hand out, shivering when it touched the golden glow of her palm. Magic streaked up my arm, sparkling and bright.

Damn, she was powerful.

The seer gasped. "Exactly as I expected." Her head tilted up until I could feel her gaze on me. "This *is* a big problem."

Told you. I bit my tongue on the words, obviously. Even I was smart enough not to piss off the Great One before she'd told me the good stuff. "Do you know how to help me?"

"No."

"Then why did you call me here? I'm at a dead end. I can't find the Titans, and even if I do, I don't know how to stop them. I hoped you'd have answers."

"I can point you in the right direction." She squeezed my hand. "I can feel something within you. A bit of magical Morse code that the Titans placed there when you saw them last."

"Magical Morse code?"

"It's like a connection with your soul. In the Greek Pantheon, powerful beings are all connected. When you met the Titans, the connection ignited. It's like a calling card, and they'd like to speak to you."

A jolt of cold fear raced through me. "Why are you only telling me now? Couldn't you have contacted me sooner?"

"Because I didn't know about it before. I'm a magical conduit, and they've used me to call you to them. I think they knew you had access to me because you are an Amazon."

"What do you mean, *call me to them*? I don't want to go to them." And why had they waited until *now*?

"You must. If you want answers, it's your only choice." Before I could so much as blink, she reached up and touched my forehead. "Sleep."

Panic flared in my chest, and my heart nearly broke through my ribs. I wanted to get up and charge away from her, but my muscles had stopped working. Within a half second, I collapsed to my back, sleep stealing over my consciousness.

A moment later, I blinked my eyes open.

Around me, the world was dark. Lightning flashed in the distance, an electric white light that was followed almost immediately by a thunderous boom that rattled my bones. The air stank of sulfur and death, rotten eggs along with decay.

Pure terror streaked through my veins as I climbed to my feet, my legs feeling like jelly. Stone walls towered around me, reaching high into the sky. I blinked.

Holy fates, I was standing in some kind of massive fortress. An animal instinct to run and hide streaked through my mind.

I resisted, though barely. Instinct told me that I needed to stand my ground.

I stood right next to an enormously tall wall. I'd only ever been in one other place that was so huge.

The Titans' old headquarters.

The wall itself glittered with a dark sparkle. I reached for it, but my fingers passed right through the wall. I grinned, trying again. My hand passed through the wall a second time.

Good. I wasn't really here. That might keep me alive.

I turned around and looked up, searching the tops of the

walls for guards who might be looking down upon me. They were so high up that vertigo made my head spin.

Through the darkness, I caught sight of a black stone tower spearing into the air. There was a huge golden crystal sitting atop it. The thing sparkled despite the darkness, and magic radiated from it.

But what the hell was it?

"The little rat has arrived." The voice boomed through the courtyard, vibrating through me.

Who the hell was speaking?

And were they talking about me?

I searched for the voice.

Three massive figures stepped through the darkness at the other end of the massive courtyard.

The Titans.

I swallowed hard, my skin ice cold.

Cronus, Crius, and Theia. The three of them stood at least fifty feet tall, each wearing fine golden armor. They were all attractive in a terrifying way—true gods. Cronus wore a huge crown, while Crius had the horns of a ram. Theia's eyes glowed with sparking light, an eerie reminder of her ability to shoot fire right out of them.

Their magic seethed around them, bringing with it the sound of battle and the feeling of death. At their feet, a horde of demons and Magica gathered. Though the demons looked normal, there was a maniacal light in the eyes of the Magica.

Oh, shit.

Just like the ones at the castle.

These were the followers they'd converted. Just like the ones we'd seen at their island fortress, except so many more.

"You think you've defeated us?" Cronus bellowed. His golden crown gleamed beneath the lightning.

His voice shook my bones, but I stiffened my spine. "Well,

not yet." I shrugged as if I didn't care. I totally care. "But we're going to. Soon."

He barked a laugh, and I couldn't sense even the tiniest bit of bravado or worry in the sound. He was pure confidence, and it made me even more nervous.

"Why am I here?" I demanded.

"We await you."

"What the hell does that even mean?"

He made a sweeping gesture with his hand. "It's quite obvious. You have become an annoyance, and we would like to eliminate you."

In the old myths, Cronus had eaten all of his children because a prophecy had said that one would overthrow him. So he was clearly a guy who liked to get out ahead of the problem. Only this time, he wanted to eat me.

"Is that why you sent an army to the Protectorate castle?" I asked.

Theia nodded. "You're clever enough not to walk out into their arms." Her expression said that I was barely clever enough. "But we wanted to encourage you. Your life will never be the same again, so come to us. Defeat us."

A laugh echoed through her words, indicating how unlikely she thought that was. I didn't bother reminding her that I'd nearly beaten her last time. I'd gotten so close that they'd run for it.

"We will give you the location of this fortress," Cronus said. "It is your fate to come here and fight us. Finish it."

An image flashed inside my mind—a map, with a little white dot flaring brightly. It was the location of this fortress, and suddenly, I knew exactly where we were. I could navigate my way back here.

Cool. Except...

This was totally a trap. No way they'd make it so easy for me.

"So, let me get this straight. You want to get rid of me, so you've invited me to your fortress."

Crius nodded, his large horns bobbing. "Precisely."

"This is obviously a trap."

Cronus shrugged. "Clearly. We intend to win and kill you." He swept his hand out. "And we have a huge army with which to do it."

"Why would I ever come here if certain death is waiting for me?"

"You are fated to be the only one who can stop us, and you know it. It is your duty, and you wouldn't want to ignore that, would you?"

I didn't want to, no, but I couldn't make this easy for them. "Hmmm. I'm just not finding a lot of incentive here, to be honest. I don't want to walk into a death trap. And anyway, from what I can tell, you're holed up here. Hiding. Not that big of a threat."

Theia's face twisted. "We are amassing an army."

"How? I bound your dark magic so that it can't pollute the world and turn more people." Though they'd managed to create a pretty big army before I'd put a halt to their plans, unfortunately.

"We are crafting a counter-spell," Cronus said. "Soon, we will have all of the things we need for it. And when we do, our dark magic will explode outward with greater force than ever before. It will convert everyone to our side and turn the world to darkness and chaos. And *they will worship us*."

Unease rippled through me. Could that be true? "Why are you telling me your whole evil plan? That seems really short-sighted. Why don't you just wait until this fancy counter-spell is completed?"

"To encourage you to come to us." Crius glowered, his horns nearly vibrating with annoyance.

They were really obsessed with getting me to come to them. Enough so they were laying out their whole plan as incentive to get me here faster.

I didn't believe a word of it. This whole thing smelled fishy.

There was a lot more to this than they were saying, and I needed to figure it the hell out.

I tapped my foot as I stared at them, making sure to take in every detail that I could. I was incorporeal now, so they clearly couldn't hurt me. If they could, they would have. Did that mean I could wander around and look for weak spots in their fortress?

Probably not. But if I could sneak away, it was definitely on my to-do list.

Because I was coming back here. I just needed to figure out what their angle was, and how to defeat them. They were packing some major magical heat, and I'd be mincemeat if I came back unprepared.

I was debating how to sneak away from them when Cronus waved his hand and boomed, "Begone!"

A moment later, my consciousness winked out of existence. There was blackness for a millisecond, then I gasped.

Bright light surrounded me, and I sat up. A golden glow to my left caught my eye, and I turned.

The Great One.

She leaned toward me, her interest palpable. "Well, what did you learn?"

"The Titans want me to come to them." I told her the whole story, finishing with, "Am I really the only one who can defeat them?"

She nodded, her aura turning a somber gray. "Indeed, that is what is fated."

Crap.

I didn't mind the risk. But what if I failed? They were already fixated on me. That was going to make it so much harder. "But how am I supposed to do that? There are three of them, and they're massively powerful. Way more powerful than I am."

"Are they, though? You haven't even fully come into your powers."

"I haven't?" I'd gotten a lot of Dragon God powers lately. There were even more?

"No, indeed not." She reached for my hand again, and I let her grip it tightly. Warmth glowed from her palm to my own. "You have one last transition. *See*."

The command echoed through me, tugging at my insides. Recognition flared within me, and a sense of home.

I closed my eyes, and a vision flashed on the inside of my eyelids. Fire burst in front of me, as if it had surged out of me. The ground fell away below.

Was I flying?

Holy fates, I felt like I was flying.

I soared on the breeze, powerful and strong.

But what was I?

Ana was the Morrigan, a giant Celtic crow, and Bree a Valkyrie.

I had no idea what I was.

This was my future, though. I could feel it so strongly.

A moment later, I returned to myself. I was no longer flying through the air, mysterious and strong. I was sitting with the Great One in the field.

"What will I become?" I asked.

An enigmatic smile crossed her face. "That is for you to determine."

"How, though?"

"You must go to Mount Olympus. There, you will find your final powers. Prove yourself worthy, and you will gain the strength to defeat the Titans."

Okay, I could work with this. I wasn't strong enough now to

take them out, but I could be. That was hope, and I would cling to it.

I liked having a goal. An answer.

"Is there anything else you can tell me about what I will face?"

"Be brave." The seer reached out and touched my chest, right over my heart. Warmth flared within me, and a moment later, the ether sucked me in, dragging me back toward the Amazons.

I arrived back at the Amazons' headquarters, panting. It took everything I had to stay on my feet, and I swayed as I turned.

The first thing I saw in the basement room was the portal. It still flickered red and black. My stomach lurched at the memory of what I'd just been through, and I turned from it.

The queens stood on the other side of the room, seeming to be holding a conversation with Romeo. Poppy and Eloise were stretched out on their backs, clearly snoozing.

As if they sensed me, Queens Penthesilea and Hippolyta turned to me.

"Well?" Queen Penthesilea asked.

"The Titans called me to them. I saw them."

Their jaws dropped, and I explained what had happened as I approached. They both frowned.

"That's quite bold, isn't it?" Queen Hippolyta said. "Asking you to come to them."

"It is. And even if I do go to them and manage to defeat them, we still haven't figured out how to put them back in Tartarus."

"We've been working on a solution to that," Queen Penthesilea said. "We might have something soon."

"Oh, thank fates." Another worry tugged at me. "How the hell do I get to Mount Olympus? Do I just...*climb*?"

"You can," Queen Hippolyta said. "But that won't take you to the mountain of the gods. You need to go the back way, through the magical realm."

"How do I get there?"

"You'll need a guide," Queen Penthesilea said. "Even we don't dare go there. But there are two who could lead you. Prometheus and Atlas."

"The last of the Titans?" The only two who weren't evil and hadn't been thrown in Tartarus.

"The very same." Queen Hippolyta frowned. "Atlas will surely be too busy. His work keeping the heavens and satellites in order is too demanding. But for the right price, Prometheus will take you."

I frowned at the memory of the surly, drunken Titan. *That* was my best bet? "There's no one else?"

"Not that I know of." Queen Hippolyta looked at Queen Penthesilea . "Any other ideas?"

She shook her head. "Just convince him of your plight. He might demand a price, but I do believe he will help you."

I freaking hoped so.

My comms charm flared to life, and Bree's voice echoed out. "Rowan, if you're available, we need you!"

I pressed my fingertips to the charm. "Where are you? Is the army attacking?"

"No, they're stable. There's a problem in the Grassmarket. By the entrance to The Vaults. Hurry."

Damn it. That was my favorite part of Edinburgh. We liked to hang out in the all-magic neighborhood when we had some free time.

"I'm coming." I looked at the queens. "I need to go."

They both nodded.

"Good luck. And keep us updated," Queen Hippolyta said.

"I will." I reached out and squeezed each of their hands. Then I gently nudged Poppy and Eloise's left feet with my toe. "Wake up, guys. We're headed out of here."

As they scampered up, I dug into my pocket and withdrew the extra transport charm that Maximus had given me. I threw it to the ground and stepped inside, envisioning the Grassmarket. The Menacing Menagerie followed, and I braced myself as the ether sucked me in.

It spun me through space and spat me out into chaos. Magic blasted through the air, exploding as it hit buildings and rubbish bins. I dived into an alley and squeezed myself up against the rough stone wall. It was dark, the light of dawn barely penetrating the alley.

Another blast of magic plowed right in front of my face. It was so strong that it slammed my head back against the stone. Pain flared, bright and fierce, and the magic continued on, hurtling down the alley to explode against a puddle. Wet, slimy water slapped across my cheeks, and I winced. I didn't dare stick my head out, not yet.

The Menacing Menagerie huddled around my ankles. Romeo was so low to the ground that the blasts of deadly magic flew right over his head. He peeked out around the side of the building. Poppy and Eloise jostled for a look as well.

"What do you see?" I whispered.

We're at the end of the Grassmarket, near the entrance to The Vaults. There's five, no seven, crazy mages with bright eyes. They're throwing magic at the buildings. Trying to destroy them.

"Why the hell would they want to do that?"

Beats me. Jude, Bree, and Caro are fending them off, but the enemy is strong.

The sound of thunder cracked through the dawn—Bree throwing her lightning, no doubt.

A stream of pink water flowed into the alley, edging around my boots. It had to come from Caro's water magic. She liked to shoot powerful jets of water straight through demons' chests. It always came out pink on the other side.

"I need to get out there." Another blast of magic plowed in front of my face. Someone had obviously seen me arrive, and now they were pinning me down. "Do you see the guy throwing sonic booms at me?"

Romeo peered hard into the street. *Left, other side of the street. Near the big oak. He's partially behind the trunk.*

I sucked in a deep breath, envisioning the huge oak that stood in the middle of the sidewalk. The thing was ancient. I didn't want to hit it with any of my magic.

I dug into my potion bag, withdrawing a glass bomb filled with a stunner. It was smooth against my palm, comforting.

"Tell me when he pops out to throw some magic." I'd only have a second before the blast reached me, so I'd have to be damned fast.

Tension thrummed along my muscles as I gripped the glass ball lightly.

Now!

I lunged out from behind the corner of the wall, immediately spotting the figure who had his hands raised to throw a blast of deadly magic at me. His dark hair waved back from his face, wild and messy. A crazed light gleamed in his bright eyes, and the long black trench coat he wore was entirely nondescript.

I hurled my potion bomb at him just as he released a jet of sonic boom. I made sure to aim high so it would miss the boom and arc down upon him. The glass ball flew through the morning air, glinting in the pale sun.

I dived low, feeling the blast of his magic ripple my hair as I slammed into the stone ground. I peeked up just in time to see my potion bomb smash into his shoulder. He'd tried to lunge out of the way, but he'd been too slow.

The glass shattered, showering him in blue liquid, and he stiffened before falling, a shocked expression on his face.

I rolled toward a rubbish bin on my right, and crouched behind it as I surveyed the scene. It looked just as Romeo had described. The attackers appeared to have come from The Vaults and were now targeting the everyday shops in the Grassmarket. Pure chaos for the sake of chaos, since it didn't seem like they were trying to rob the places.

Caro, with her platinum bob gleaming in the dawn sun, shot fierce jets of water at two mages who stood on the other side of the street. They were fast, dodging her blasts, but she was quick in turn, avoiding their firebombs.

The Menacing Menagerie had left the safety of the alley and had lunged at the mage who stood closest to us. They were all flying fur and fangs, claws glinting in the light. The mage shrieked in terror and pain, and I was glad the Menagerie was on my side. The pure delight on Eloise's face was creepy, frankly, and Poppy was so into the attack that she'd lost her flower.

Jude stood on my side of the street, cracking her electric whip at a man who waved his arms, disrupting the bricks beneath her feet. They rose into the air, swirling around Jude, threatening to slam into her. She raised her free hand, casting a sparkling, protective shield around herself as she cracked her whip at the man.

Her whip twined around his body, and he screamed. The bricks dropped, and I looked away, searching for Bree.

She flew high in the sky, her silver wings gleaming, as she shot lightning bolts at the three remaining attackers below.

Death from above.

There was a guy in the middle of the street who seemed to

be the most powerful. His eyes gleamed the brightest, and he looked like a true fanatic.

Bree's lightning bolts didn't seem to have much effect on him. He almost absorbed them.

I needed to try my sun magic against him. If it'd been strong enough to hurt the Titans, this guy didn't stand a chance. "Bree! I've got him!"

Bree's gaze flashed to me, and she nodded, then turned her attention to the other two.

I raised my hands and lined the mage up in my sights. His black trench coat whipped around his legs on an unnatural wind, and his hair flew back from his face. Actual flames shined within his eyes, and when he turned to me, I had a quick vision of a massive fireball coming my way.

As I called upon the magic of the sun, the man raised his hands.

Yep, he was *definitely* about to throw a giant fireball my way.

His magic swelled on the air, stinking of rot and decay. Red light glowed around his hands. As the huge ball of flame flew toward me, I lunged left, barely avoiding it.

The sun's power sizzled within me, difficult to control, and I unleashed it, sending it at the mage. The magic slammed into him, lighting him up like a firework.

Holy fates!

He shook and fell, collapsing to the ground like a sack of rocks.

I stared down at my hands. That was different than the sun magic I'd used against the Titans. Without a doubt, this was a magic I needed to explore more.

The remaining mages—there were only three of them now —all faltered at the sight of their leader on the ground. I darted toward the one nearest me, a young guy with big glasses and a sweater vest. He really didn't look like the sort who should be participating in an attack on innocent businesses. He should be working in an IT department or a chemistry lab right now.

I grabbed the guy around the collar, yanking him around to face me. As hard as I could, I slammed him against the brick wall.

Shock widened his dark eyes, which gleamed with the light of a fanatic.

"What the hell are you doing?" I asked. "Attacking businesses like some loser?"

He scowled. "I'm not a loser."

"*That's* the part you focus on?" I shook him hard, calling upon a dagger from the ether and pressing it against his belly. "I could kill you here and now, and you're concerned that I called you a loser?"

He scowled at me, his lips twisting over perfect white teeth.

I shook him again. "Does this have anything to do with the Titans?"

"They make a compelling point." He shrugged, then winced when my dagger pressed a little deeper into his stomach.

"Mind control?" I shook him. "Can you feel them in your mind? Did their magic turn yours dark?"

The kid laughed, an ugly sound. "No mind control. *I'm* the one in control of me."

"Then why the hell are you doing this?"

"Yesterday, that guy"—he pointed to the fallen mage who I thought was the leader—"came up to me and presented a compelling argument about the Titans."

"Yesterday?" What the hell? Five days ago, we'd bound the Titans dark magic from spreading and converting people from light magic to dark. And this guy was a new recruit as of yesterday? "What the hell was his compelling argument?"

"Chaos." The kid grinned, crazy as a loon. "The Titans are going to rise up and take over the earth. Chaos is coming, and we'll worship them. So we thought we'd start early. Join their cause and prove we're loyal."

"By blowing up a fish and chips shop?" I jerked my head toward the shop window to his left, then shook my head, disgusted. "You could kill people."

"So?" The lack of concern on the kid's face was chilling. And actually, I needed to stop calling him a kid. He was my age.

And he'd made the decision to do this of his own free will.

What a little shit.

I was so pissed I almost didn't notice his hand rising, glowing red with flame. He slapped it toward my face, going for a kill shot. I shoved my dagger into his side and smacked his hand away just as another dagger flew through the air and pierced the kid's hand, making the magic fizzle.

Startled, I glanced left. Maximus stood there. He'd thrown the dagger, stopping the kid from barbecuing my face.

"Right place, right time, huh?" I asked as the kid shrieked.

The corner of Maximus's mouth tilted up in a sexy smile. "Always."

"Thanks." I nodded toward the body of the leader mage that was still lying in the square. He might still be alive, which meant he could wake up at any moment. "Will you take care of that guy? Tie him up?"

Maximus nodded. "On it."

I gave the street a quick look to make sure everything was under control—it was—then turned back to the jerk who'd tried to fricassee me. His eyes were wide and his face pale. I could let him die.

But no, I really didn't like that idea. It was one thing to kill demons. I'd kill mortals if I had to, but I *didn't* have to kill this one, so I didn't want to.

I yanked my blade out of his side, and he groaned, going to

his knees. I knelt beside him, digging around in my potion belt to find the healing tonic.

"I'm going to make sure you don't die." I jerked his head up so he was looking at me. "And the Order of the Magica will take it from here. But if you *ever* do something like this again, I will come for you."

The guy's face whitened, and I grinned, viciously satisfied. I sounded seriously scary, and the guy was totally buying it. Honestly, I didn't have the time to hunt him down, but he didn't need to know that.

I poured the potion onto his wound, and it sizzled with a pale blue smoke. The guy relaxed as the wound knit itself back together.

"Want me to take him?" Caro's voice sounded from behind me. "I've got restraints."

I stood, glaring at the guy, who didn't move, then looked at my friend. "Thanks, Caro."

"I got your back, pal." She grinned.

I smiled. It was nice to have friends who cared. So much of my life recently had been spent in darkness, alone. It was really turning around now, but it'd only stay that way if I could take out the Titans. And soon.

A quick glance at Maximus showed that he'd trussed up the leader with some shackles he'd conjured. He had the guy gripped by his collar, and stood waiting for Jude's orders.

Everyone else seemed dead. Since they weren't demons, their bodies weren't disappearing like a demon's would. I frowned, my stomach turning.

I didn't like this, not one little bit.

3

Across the street, Jude spoke into her comms charm. A moment later, several figures appeared from the alley that contained the portal back to the Protectorate castle.

Bree landed next to me, folding her silver wings into her body. "Clean-up crew."

"What a waste." These guys had been a bunch of idiots and assholes, but still, it was a shame they'd turned to the dark side and died as a result.

"What the hell were they doing?" Bree asked, shoving her shiny dark hair back off her face. "You talked to one, right, Rowan?"

"Yeah. And they weren't mind controlled by the Titans. I don't think their magic was even turned dark by them."

"What do you mean?" Bree frowned.

"They chose to do this. Anarchists or rebels or what the hell ever. Apparently, they joined the Titan's cause willingly."

"So it's worse than we thought."

"I think so." I searched for Jude and Maximus, who were directing the clean-up crew. When Jude turned to me, I waved her over.

"What's going on?" Bree asked, clearly reading something in my expression. "Did you learn something useful at the Amazons'?"

"I did, but let's talk it out together. Jude's coming this way now."

Jude stopped next to us. "I think we all need to sit down and regroup. Figure out what the heck is going on."

Fates, did I. Just one little rest would be divine.

"Whiskey and Warlock?" Bree asked. "It's the closest place that's quiet."

"Perfect," Jude said.

Maximus joined us, and we walked down the street toward the pub.

We entered the cozy interior of the Whiskey and Warlock. It wasn't technically open yet—too early—but as expected, Sophie was behind the bar. She lived above it, and no doubt she'd heard the commotion in the street.

Worry glinted in her green eyes, and her red hair was messy from sleep. She still wore her PJs, which were emblazoned with the slogan *Highland Cow Hair, Don't Care.*

"Is everything okay out there?" She twisted a rag in her hands.

"Fine, now," Jude said. "Could we trouble you for some coffee?"

Sophie nodded, looking almost grateful to have a task, and turned back to the bar. "Be right out in a jiffy."

We took our usual seats in front of the fire, which was now banked. Without the gleaming golden light shining on the copper mugs that hung from the ceiling, the place felt like it was asleep. The chill in the air made me tuck deeper into my jacket, and I leaned my shoulder against Maximus's.

Briefly, I told them what I'd learned from the punk I'd cornered in the street.

Jude rubbed her forehead, her starry blue eyes weary. Her dark braids were pulled back from her face, and as usual, it looked like it'd been a while since she'd slept. "This is just getting worse."

"Much worse." I frowned. "And I think it will keep happening."

"It will," Maximus said. "Chaos begets more chaos."

"We need to stop the Titans," Bree said. "They're the key."

She was right.

Sophie arrived at our table and set down a tray of coffee mugs. There was also a plate of scones and butter and jam. She smiled apologetically. "They're just from the shop down the corner. Pre-made. But they're all we've got."

I grabbed a scone greedily, my stomach growling. "They look fantastic."

I took a big bite, not bothering with the butter and jam. They were a little dry, but I couldn't have cared less.

After I swallowed, Jude caught my eye. "What did you learn from the Amazons?"

"Ah, that." I set the scone down. "You'll be surprised."

She raised her dark brows.

"The Titans told me where they are."

"What?" A chorus sounded from around the table.

"They *told* you?" Bree asked, incredulous.

"Yep. Apparently when I was with them last, they created some kind of connection with my soul. It allows them to deliver a message to me whenever they want to."

"They waited until now, so they were clearly preparing for something," Maximus said.

"And the message was their location?" Jude asked. "Why the hell would they give that up?"

"They want me for something. Maybe just to kill me, but I think it's more."

Power of Magic 35

"They sent the army to the gates for you," Bree said.

"Incentive to come to them. They want me to fight them, and they say they plan to kill me."

"But to give up their location?" Jude asked. "That's insane."

"They're confident," I said. "I don't think they can catch me otherwise—they can't get through the castle walls, after all. And I'm always on the move, so catching me is hard."

"They know we don't have the numbers to defeat them." Bree scowled.

"Not yet." A grim expression crossed Maximus's face. "We'll need an army."

"Definitely." I described the number of people I'd seen in the compound. "And they're about to collect more followers. They're working on a spell that will release their dark magic again. There's so much of it inside them that they would convert the earth to evil, all in one fell swoop. And they'll be worshipped again—I think that's a big deal to them."

"What kind of spell?" Jude asked.

"Just a sec." I got up and asked Sophie for a pen and paper, then sat down and drew the golden crystal contraption I'd seen on the top of their tower. "I think this is part of their plan, but they need more ingredients for the spell to make that thing work."

"They just told you all of this?" Jude asked, skeptical. "They sound like villains laying out their plan in some bad movie."

I nodded. "I know. It's weird."

"It could be as straightforward as it seems," Maximus said. "They want to kill you so they draw you to them. But I doubt it. They want you for something. They want you badly enough that they invited you. Knowing that you could bring an army."

"It's going to have to be a big army." Bree sat back, her expression grim. "But you can't go to their fortress. No way."

"According to the Amazons' Great One, I'm the only one who can defeat the Titans."

"Fate decrees it." Jude scowled. "But it's so risky."

"It's risky for everyone," I said.

She rubbed a hand over her face again, weariness personified. "We need to figure out what that contraption is."

Maximus pulled my drawing toward him, studying it. "You said the crystal was golden and that it rotated?"

I nodded.

"I think it's a bind-breaking device. It'll destroy the magic on their binding. But it can't be strong enough to destroy the spell we placed on them." He sighed. "Unless they have a powerful enough power source."

"There aren't many of those in existence," Jude said. "Most are protected by the Order of the Magica."

"I've heard of one in Thailand. An ancient one." He shook his head. "But even it may not be strong enough."

"We need to go get it anyway," Bree said. "Beat them to it."

Jude nodded. "You go, Bree. You're fast. Bring Ana with you for safety." She looked at Maximus. "Can you tell them how to get there?"

"I can provide a bit of direction, but not everything you need."

"I got it." Bree grinned, ruthless. "Nothing will stop me."

"Good. If you can get it before them, it will seriously slow them down. We need to raise an army before they complete their device and release their power."

"If only our binding spell had been stronger," I said.

"We bought ourselves time we desperately needed." Jude looked at me. "And what's your plan? You clearly still have something on your mind."

I nodded. "I have to go to Mount Olympus to complete my

transformation to Dragon God. Only then will I be strong enough to defeat the Titans."

Jude nodded, a smile spreading across her face. "I like the sound of that."

"More magic is always good." Though I felt like I was about to burst at the seams, I had so much magic now. I looked at Maximus. "Will you come as backup?"

He nodded. "Of course."

"Good." Jude nodded. "We'll work on getting that power source before they do and growing an army. When you've completed your transition, Rowan, we'll attack. But be fast. We're running out of time."

Jude was so right about that. I could feel it pressing on my shoulders. The Titans had been clever about their offer, seeding it with just enough urgency and hope to really get me moving.

I was going to have to be cleverer than they were, that was for sure. Or we were screwed.

An hour later, Maximus and I stood outside of the bar where I'd first met Prometheus. I'd needed to collect a few more healing potions to replace the ones I'd used, and we'd wanted to give Prometheus time to get to his favorite bar. It was three hours ahead in Istanbul, so it was nearly noon here.

The Menacing Menagerie sat at my feet, clearly unwilling to let me go it alone here.

Maximus looked at me, his brow creased with concern. "You sure you're okay? That was a nasty fight back there."

"Fine." I smiled at him. "Let's go around back. I have an idea."

He nodded, and followed me through the narrow alley at the

side of the building. The back entrance was unguarded. Just a heavy wooden door with a few rubbish bins next to it.

I leaned up to whisper in Maximus's ear. "I'm going to try to talk to the waitress real quick. Will you wait here?"

He nodded.

I looked down at Romeo, Eloise, and Poppy. "Hang out here, okay? I don't know how they feel about critters in the kitchen."

All three of them looked dreadfully offended, and I gave them an apologetic smile.

Romeo huffed. *Fine, then.*

I pushed open the door and stepped into the dimly lit hallway. My eyes adjusted, and I scanned the space, spotting the doorways to the bathrooms. This was the hallway I'd come into before when I'd needed to take my Sober Up potion. The entrance to the bar was about six feet away, and I crept up, peering inside.

Little tables crowded the space, but they were mostly empty. Prometheus sat at the same table he'd occupied last time I'd found him. He was as big and imposing as ever, but this time, he was far soberer. His clothes were clean and tidy, his face shaved and his dark hair swept back from his forehead. He sat hunched over a notebook, scrawling something. A small cup of steaming coffee sat at his elbow.

Yep.

My suspicions weren't fully confirmed, but I was getting there. When I'd met him last, I'd taken him to be a drunk and worked on that assumption, trying to drink him under the table.

I'd been successful—sort of. I'd ended up with the info I'd wanted and a massive hangover. But I wasn't entirely convinced he'd been the drunk I thought he was. I was even less convinced now. He looked pretty dang sober.

I hurried toward the fourth door in the hallway. It was shut, but if my guess was correct, it led to the kitchen.

I slipped inside, grinning at the sight of a cook quickly chopping vegetables behind a counter. He scowled at me.

"Can I speak to the waitress?" I asked.

He scowled again, but I spotted the same dark-haired woman who'd served our drinks when I'd been here last. She was fiddling with a strange little pot that steamed, and I hurried to her.

I stopped at her side, and she looked up, startled.

"Ayse, you need help?" the cook asked.

The waitress turned back to him. "I'm fine." She looked at me. "What do you want?"

Magic sparked about her, a signature that I hadn't noticed before. It smelled of lavender and felt like cold snow falling on my face. She was far more powerful than I'd realized.

I squinted at her. "You're not a regular waitress."

She arched a dark brow. "And you're not a regular patron."

I tried to get a better hit of her signature, but she locked it down tight. She was hiding something, but maybe it wasn't my business.

"What do you want?" she asked.

"Just to ask some questions."

"That's what they all say." She shook her head. "Trouble usually follows."

"I can't argue that. But I'm trying to get ahead of the trouble." I tilted my head toward the bar. "The man who is in here all the time. He's not a drunk, is he?"

She shrugged, but there was knowledge in her eyes.

The more I thought about it, the more this seemed like some kind of secret supernatural headquarters for something. The kind where people pretended to be normal—a waitress, a drunken patron—while actually doing something far more important.

I glanced at the cook, but he was ignoring me now. Without getting closer, I couldn't figure out if he had any magic.

"I think this place isn't what it seems," I said. "And I think Prometheus was helping me last time I was here. Beyond just giving me info because I drank it out of him."

"Maybe he was."

"So if I went out there now, he might help me again? Without me having to drink him under the table?"

The corner of her mouth pulled up in a smile, and she stifled a laugh. "You were quite the sight last time."

"I was a moron last time." I'd made an assumption about Prometheus that had come back to bite me in the butt. "But I won't be a moron this time."

She shrugged. "Maybe you won't be." She leaned close. "But if you really need his help, and he's resisting, remind him of his debt to humanity."

"Debt?"

"He gave man fire. It was a blessing and a curse, leading us from our blissful youth in the dark into the light of adulthood."

"What do you mean, exactly?"

"Fire brought many gifts. But it also brought war and greed and rage. He feels guilt over that."

I remembered the myth. Prometheus had been the one to gift fire to the humans. He'd been punished for centuries, tied to a rock where an eagle ate his liver over and over again.

"Thanks." I made a circular motion with my index finger, indicating the restaurant. "Good luck with whatever it is you do here."

"Just saving the world." She raised a little cup. "One coffee at a time."

Yeah, something important was definitely going on here. I stopped by the alley to grab Maximus and the Menacing Menagerie, then we entered the bar.

Prometheus looked up as soon as we entered, his eyes narrowing. I smiled and waved, weaving my way between the tiny tables until I reached his.

"Mind if I join you?"

He waved his hand to indicate the chairs. "I doubt I have a choice."

"Well, no. I do have to ask you for something." I pulled out a chair for the Menagerie, and they all climbed on. Then I sat on my own.

His mouth flattened and he nodded, then he looked at Maximus. "You were here the other night as well, weren't you? When she tried to drink me under the table."

"Succeeded," I said.

He shrugged. "But only because I let you."

Maximus sat and stuck his hand out. "Maximus Valerius."

They shook, and Prometheus looked at the Menagerie. "Who are you?"

"The Menacing Menagerie," I said. "Formerly the Magical Menagerie, greatest all-animal circus in Europe."

Prometheus's brows rose. "You must be skilled."

The three nodded.

Prometheus looked between Maximus and me. "What do you want now?"

"I need a guide up Mount Olympus, and I've been told you're the guy."

"Me or Atlas. Go bother him."

"He's busy." And damned hard to find.

"So am I." He indicated his notebook, and I looked at it. The scribbling writing disappeared as soon as my gaze fell upon it.

"Nice trick."

He grinned. "I'm full of them."

I leaned closer. "I really need your help." As quickly as I could, I explained the threat of the Titans.

"Those bastards?" he asked. "I knew they were making a fuss about rising."

"Will you help us, then?" Maximus asked.

"What will you do for me?"

"It's not so much what we'll do for each other," I said. "It's more what we'll do for the world."

He scoffed.

"I know you care," I said. "And I think you're some kind of secret operative who does good deeds."

He looked at me like I was nuts. "Like help old ladies across the street?"

"On a bigger scale."

He scowled, expression skeptical, but I could tell there was more to him. So I pulled out the big guns. "I was told to remind you of your debt to the world."

His scowl only deepened. His gaze flicked toward the kitchen, where I assumed Ayse was watching. He was clearly considering it, and I held my breath.

"Fine." He held up a hand. "But on one condition. After this is over, I'd like the help of your friends there." He pointed to the Menagerie. "With one little thing."

"Is it dangerous?" I demanded.

Eloise perked up at the idea, and I knew that if he said yes, she'd only be more inclined to help.

"A bit, yes."

We'll do it.

I glared at Romeo.

He shrugged. *We make up our own minds. We'll help the big man so he'll help you. Easy peasy.*

"It looks like they've agreed," I said.

A satisfied smile sliced across Prometheus's face. "Good."

"Can we get started now?" I asked.

"After lunch."

"Can we have it on the go?"

He sighed, then nodded. "I rarely let anything get in the way of my stomach, you know. It's no way to live."

"Fair enough."

He polished off his coffee, shoved his notebook in the pocket of his dark canvas jacket, and stood. He was one of the few people I'd ever met who was as tall as Maximus. Between them and the Menagerie, I had some good backup for Mount Olympus.

We swung by the kitchen, where we each picked up a savory pita filled with steaming meat. Even the Menagerie took one despite the fact that it hadn't been in the bin first.

We ate in silence as we walked out onto the street. Prometheus polished his off in less than a minute, then turned to look at us. "It's good news for you that I can transport."

"Fantastic."

"The less good news is that it's not a fun journey." He grinned, and it was just a little bit evil.

"We don't go via the ether?" Maximus asked.

"Sorta." His smiled widened, and he used his hand to draw a large circle in the air. The space filled with dark smoke, and a cold wind emitted from it. "Come on."

He leapt into the circle, disappearing immediately.

"Crap." I scowled at the portal.

Maximus didn't hesitate. Just stepped in.

Romeo looked up at me. *We'll see you later.*

"Wimp."

He grinned, little fangs gleaming white. *Smart.*

I couldn't argue with that. I gave the Menagerie a quick salute, ate the last bite of my pita, then jumped into the portal before it disappeared.

Instead of being sucked into the ether, I fell, hurtling through space as if I'd jumped off a cliff. Icy wind blasted by me as I plummeted through the cold air. A scream tore from my lips, and my stomach leapt into my throat. My hair whipped around my face and my eyes watered.

Holy fates, had we been tricked?

I tried calling on my magic, desperate to develop some kind of flying skill. And where was Maximus?

I tried looking down, but I couldn't see anything. Just open sky and clouds as the cold wind nearly blinded me.

Oh fates, I am going to die.

4

All I could hear was my scream as I fell. I shrieked like a banshee, unable to stop myself. I fell for an eternity, or so it seemed.

Prometheus's portal jerked me to a stop, as if I were tied to an invisible bungee cord. I blinked, my eyes watering, and realized that I was near the ground, floating slowly toward it. Prometheus's portal was one hell of a ride.

I looked down, spotting Prometheus and Maximus standing on the ground. Maximus was white as a sheet, and an enormous inflatable mattress sat next to him. Clearly something he'd conjured.

Prometheus grinned up at me like a maniac. "Fun, huh?"

My feet hit the ground gently, and my stomach retreated to its proper place in my abdomen. I growled at Prometheus. "Jerk."

He shrugged, a fake-innocent look on his face. "I warned you."

"Not well enough."

"The Menagerie was too smart to come?" Maximus asked.

"Yep."

I turned in a circle, inspecting our surroundings. We were at the base of a massive mountain. Olympus soared into the sky, surrounded by clouds at the top. Down here, there was dusty ground and scrub brush. Slightly farther up were huge gray rock formations that I didn't like the look of.

Maximus touched the huge inflatable mattress and it disappeared.

"Quick thinking," I said.

"I probably would have bounced pretty far if Prometheus's portal didn't have the built-in brakes." He shrugged, his expression rueful. "But it was the best I could come up with on short notice."

"At least you'd have lived." I'd have hit the ground and splatted like a bug.

Not one of my finest moments.

"You two done flirting?" Prometheus asked.

"Never." I turned to him, grinning. "We'll flirt even more if it will annoy you."

He cracked a smile.

Dang. I liked this jerk. It felt a bit like my relationship with Connor. Like Prometheus was my annoying brother or something. Maybe we were connected somehow. Him being a Greek Titan and me being the Greek Dragon God.

Ah, well. No time to dwell on it.

I looked up at the mountain. We had a long way to go. "I don't suppose there are any shortcuts? No portals?"

"The gods don't like to be disturbed, so they don't make it easy." Prometheus shrugged. "Ten thousand mortals climb the human side every year and pose for pictures. No one ever climbs this way. It's been centuries."

"No one wants to visit the gods?"

"Not often, these days. The religion is essentially dead.

Besides, they're jerks." A sour smile striped Prometheus's face. "No one would know better than I."

He was still holding a grudge about Zeus tying him up so an eagle could eat his liver every day. I couldn't blame him. I had some conflicted feelings about the Greek gods myself.

We continued up the sloping mountainside, which grew steeper as we ascended. Ahead of us, Prometheus stopped abruptly, raising his hand to indicate that we should do the same. I joined him, staring down into a deep gorge. A wild river rushed below, and there was no passage across as far as I could see. The gorge was at least a hundred meters across.

"Got a plan?" I asked.

"We wait." Prometheus's brow was set in deep creases.

I glanced at Maximus, who shrugged. We only waited a moment, however, before the air sparkled with magic. It rolled over me, powerful and strong, heralding the arrival of a god.

"Who's coming?" I asked.

"The Guardian of the Gate." As soon as the words left Prometheus's mouth, Hermes appeared.

He stood at the edge of the gorge, his golden hair a match with the winged shoes on his feet. Both gleamed brightly, along with the white tunic he wore.

"I wondered when I'd be seeing you," he said.

The messenger god had appeared to me before, directing me to visit the Amazons for the first time. Apparently, he was also a guardian of sorts.

"May we pass?" Prometheus asked.

Hermes tapped his chin. "Well, that depends. You'll have to earn it."

"Anything," I said, determined to get this over with. I needed more power to defeat the Titans, and I wouldn't let a little thing like a god and a deadly river gorge stand in my way.

Hermes grinned brightly. "I'd be wary of making that offer to too many gods. I'm a reasonable sort, but I can't say that for the rest of them."

"What must we do to pass?" Maximus asked.

"Hmmm." Hermes looked us up and down. "It's different for everyone who wishes access, but I think yours will be a test of cleverness and wits." His gaze turned to Prometheus. "Not you, though. It's up to the two of them."

Prometheus shrugged.

"What's the test?" I asked.

"A riddle."

Ah, crap. I hated riddles.

Hermes straightened his stance and adopted a booming voice. "I look at you whenever you look at me. You see but I see not; no sight have I. I speak but have no voice; your voice is heard. My lips can only open uselessly." He bowed, finishing it off with flair.

I frowned, wracking my mind. A quick glance at Maximus showed him equally confused. Prometheus, however, fairly vibrated with excitement. His eyes were bright and his mouth tense. He looked like a guy who wanted to shout out the answer at trivia.

If only I had mind-reading powers.

But since those didn't seem to be coming any time soon, I repeated the lines of the riddle in my head. I probably muddled some of them, but it was the bit about the lips opening uselessly that finally clued me in.

"I've got it." I looked at Maximus.

He nodded. "Go for it. I've never been good at riddles."

"A mirror." I grinned triumphantly.

Hermes smiled back. "Not bad. That's a very old one, you know." He turned and gestured to the river, waving his arm so a long wooden suspension bridge appeared. It stretched over the riotous river below, swinging gently in the wind.

"Oh, come on," Prometheus said. "That's our passage?"

"It was a fairly easy riddle, so the passage will be difficult." Hermes shrugged. "Another way of proving your worth."

Nerves pricked along my skin as I stared at the suspension bridge. Hell, it was so flimsy that it looked like it was made of rotten old matches.

"Best of luck." Hermes disappeared. "You won't have long, so hurry."

"I think we're going to need it," Maximus said.

I grimaced and started forward.

"Move swiftly," Prometheus said.

"Should we go one at a time so that our weight doesn't break it?" I asked.

He shook his head. "I don't think it will stick around that long. When Hermes said we wouldn't have long, he meant it."

"Let's do this, then." I stepped onto the bridge, my skin chilling as I looked down through the wooden slats at the river below. It was hundreds of feet down, but even from up here, I could see the alligators.

Oh, fates. I was in an Indiana Jones movie.

Maximus followed me, with Prometheus bringing up the rear.

Fast as I could, I hurried across the bridge, gripping the rope railings for support. The old wooden slats creaked beneath my feet, ominous cracking noises sounding from them.

I could hear Prometheus and Maximus behind me, but I focused on the bridge. I was halfway across when it began to move. It shuddered beneath my feet, then began to undulate as if a great giant were shaking it from behind.

I turned back to look, but saw only Maximus and Prometheus.

"Hurry!" Prometheus shouted.

I turned back and picked up the pace, clinging to the rope,

and I hurried along. The bridge shook and waved so much that it was impossible to hang on. My foot slipped on a loose board, and I almost went through a gap in the slats. I gripped the ropes tight, catching myself at the last minute. Sweat dotted my brow, and I pulled myself upward and continued forward.

So close. More than halfway.

The bridge heaved even harder, thrusting me up in the air as I clung to the rope. When it slammed downward, the force of my body weight on the wooden slat caused it to crack. I plunged through the gap in the bridge, both feet kicking as I gripped the rope handrails tightly.

"Hold on!" Maximus shouted.

I stared up at my hands where I gripped the rope, spotting a frayed section. Oh no.

If Maximus joined me and gripped the rope near the frayed section, our combined weight might snap it. Especially if the wooden slats broke underneath his feet.

"Stay back! The bridge is weak here!" I kicked my legs and curled my abs, trying to get my feet up onto another wooden slat so I could pull myself up.

As I watched, the rope handrail on the left continued to unravel.

Crap. I was running out of time.

As the bridge continued to thrash in the air like waves, I tried one last gigantic heave. I got my feet up onto the wooden slats and scrambled to safety.

Relative safety.

"The bridge is breaking! Hurry!" I sprinted forward, my legs wobbly on the wooden slats.

I was nearly to the end when the bridge lost tension. My stomach dropped, and I turned back just in time to see the rope handrails snap right in front of Prometheus. He leapt and grabbed onto my side of the bridge.

The wooden slats beneath my feet fell away. I clung to the rope handrails as the bridge flew through the air, praying that Maximus and Prometheus had a good grip as well.

As we sailed toward the other side of the gorge, my stomach leapt into my throat, my skin chilling. When the rope bridge slammed into the cliff, the impact shook my entire body. Pain flared as I lost my grip. I plummeted, my hands scrabbling for purchase.

Just when I thought all was lost, Maximus grabbed my wrist, his grip iron tight. My body weight yanked hard on my arm, agony slicing in my shoulder. Beneath me, Prometheus hung onto the wooden slats.

My head spun as I reached for the rope bridge with my free hand. I latched onto it.

"Got it?" Maximus asked, voice tense.

"Yeah." The word was breathless as it escaped my lips.

He let go of my arm, and I grabbed one of the wooden slats, hanging on for dear life.

"Climb!" Prometheus shouted from below.

We did, Maximus going first since he was higher up. He moved as quick as a spider, scaling the bridge that had become a ladder. I followed, my hands sweaty and legs trembling. As I ascended, I searched for vines or roots sticking out of the cliff wall. Anything to grab onto in case the bridge broke.

Controlling plants was about the only thing I could do in this circumstance. Maybe I could make the river rise up to catch us, but there were gators in it.

Talk about out of the frying pan and into the fire.

Ahead of me, Maximus flung himself onto the edge of the cliff, then turned around and reached down for me. I grabbed his strong hand, and he yanked me up.

I flopped onto the scrubby ground like a dead fish, panting

and gasping. Maximus hauled Prometheus up, and we all lay next to each other, catching our breath as we stared at the sky.

"Holy fates, that sucked," I said.

"Simple but deadly." Prometheus sounded disgusted. "One of Hermes's favorite tricks. I bet he's on the other side, laughing his ass off."

Aching, I staggered to my feet. The terrain ahead of us was even steeper than before, with rocky outcroppings and stone formations that looked like they could hide all kinds of dangers. There was less plant growth, and the air was growing cooler as well.

Maximus and Prometheus joined me. Maximus pulled me against him, pressing a kiss to the top of my head. "Thought I might have lost you for a sec."

Prometheus strode forward, starting up the mountain.

"I was too scared to process anything." I tilted my head up to look at him, and he was white as a sheet. "Wow, that really worried you, huh?"

He looked at me like I was crazy. "Yes. The idea of losing you worries me."

"Okay, when you put it like that, I see your point." I grinned. "And likewise."

In a big way. What would I do if I lost him?

I didn't even want to think about it. We hadn't known each other long, but I knew exactly how I felt about him. And it was *serious*.

We shared one last look, then started up the mountainside after Prometheus.

"Keep a wary eye out," he said. "Olympus is riddled with monsters around the base."

"It's safer here for them, I'd imagine," Maximus said. "So many more people on earth these days that they need a place like this to hide out. And with Hermes guarding this area, it's even safer."

Prometheus nodded. "The monsters made a deal to protect the gods. So, all we've got to do is get past them."

"Oh, that's all, is it?"

Prometheus and Maximus chuckled at my wry tone. Hermes was only the first guardian, apparently. I shivered, adjusting my potions bag on my back. I could almost feel the eyes of the monsters on me as we climbed, skirting around scrub brush and rocks.

"Exactly." Prometheus sounded grim. "You're lucky I believe in your mission or I sure as hell wouldn't be here."

As we climbed, the rock formations grew up around us, creating a narrow valley for us to travel through. It was only about thirty feet wide, and the stone outcroppings rose twenty feet on either side, providing dozens of places for enemies to hide. A breeze whistled through the valley, blowing my hair back from my face.

"I feel like I'm running the gauntlet," I murmured.

"There's dark magic in the air," Maximus said.

I sniffed, trying to get a hint of it. Finally, I did. A very faint scent of old dust. It wasn't outright terrible, but it was definitely unpleasant.

"Do you know what lives around here?" I asked Prometheus.

"All sorts of things. But here specifically? No."

Magic prickled against my skin as we continued between the rocks, and I shivered again.

"Something is watching us." I could feel its eyes. I called upon Artemis's gift of animal senses, hearing a slight shifting noise to the left, about thirty feet away, high in the rocks. "To the left. There's a faint noise."

A blast of magic hurled from that direction, a glowing green streak of slime. I dived left, narrowly avoiding it, and the slime slammed into the rock on my right. The stone sizzled as the acid ate away at it.

"Oh, shit, avoid that stuff!" Prometheus lunged behind a rock.

I followed, Maximus at my side. We wedged in next to Prometheus.

"Any idea what threw that?" Maximus asked.

"If I had to bet, it's an Echidna." He peered out from behind the rock and winced. "Yep."

I shoved him aside to get a look for myself, cringing at the sight of the huge snake woman. She was gorgeous on her top half—and totally naked—but the bottom was a massive two-tailed snake. The scales gleamed a beautiful green to match her eyes. Her dark hair streamed down her back, shining in the sunlight.

She raised a hand again, and green magic glowed around her palm. She was about to throw the slime at us when she stopped and smiled.

It was an evil smile. A satisfied smile.

And it was directed at something right above our heads.

"Move!" I shouted, as instinct propelled me to lunge out of the way. I managed to glance upward as I darted away from our hiding spot.

I caught sight of another Echidna—this one with blonde hair and blue snake tails. She hurled a blast of blue magic right at the spot we'd been hiding. It slammed into the ground, a sonic boom that blasted a six-foot hole into the stone.

Thankfully, Maximus and Prometheus were quick, and they'd dived out of the way just in time.

As we scrambled away from the blue Echidna, I called upon my magic. "I'll take the blue one!"

"I've got green," Maximus shouted.

"And I'll take red," Prometheus said, just as a blast of flame hurtled toward us from a third Echidna with red hair and tails.

Maximus conjured a dagger and hurled it at the green Echidna. It flew through the air, headed straight for her. She lunged left at the last moment, and the blade lodged in her right shoulder, throwing her back. She screeched, a sound of rage and pain, and I had a feeling that wasn't the last we'd see of her.

I spun to throw my potion bomb at the blue Echidna. My aim was good, but she was fast, darting out of the way. She made her green-tailed sister look like a sloth.

She threw another sonic boom, this one bigger than the last. I lunged right, avoiding the worst of it. The edge of the boom caught me in the legs, and pain flared. My limbs went numb, and I dragged myself over the ground, clawing my way to a rock outcropping that could serve as cover.

Blood pounded in my head as I debated my options. No way I could accurately throw a potion bomb when I was in this shape, and she was too fast anyway. I needed something else.

I peeked out from behind the rock, eyeing her. She stood on a stone ledge, about twenty feet away. I called upon my new gift of lightning, feeling it crackle and burn inside me.

It exploded from the sky, shooting downward to pierce the Echidna. She lit up like a lamp post, then laughed, clearly delighted.

Crap!

To my right, Prometheus stood out in the open. He raised his hands, and magic sparked around him, hot and fierce. It exploded outward, a massive wall of flame that surged toward the three Echidna, coming from all sides. He was going for all of them, and the amount of fire he produced was astonishing.

It was an inferno that surrounded us, twenty feet tall and rolling like a tsunami over the three Echidna and the rocks that surrounded them.

Heck yeah.

"Where were you hiding that?" I asked. One blast of his fire and we were home free.

A cocky smile tugged at the corner of Prometheus's mouth. "Just a little something I had saved up."

A half second later, a triumphant shriek sounded from within the flames.

"Oh, shit." Prometheus frowned. "I think they like it."

The laughter continued.

"Yeah, they do." And we were screwed.

5

"Run," Maximus said. "Our only hope is to make it through the gauntlet before they can see through the flames."

He took off, sprinting down the valley that had formed between the rocks. Prometheus and I followed.

My lungs burned as I ran, going as fast as I could on my wobbly legs. The Echidna's sonic boom had done a real number on me. "Keep up the fire, Prometheus."

If anything, it gave us a bit of cover until the Echidna reached the edge of the wall of flame and could see us.

I darted around rocks and leapt over fallen logs, running like my tail was on fire. Hell, it almost was.

But I was still too slow. I felt like Usain Bolt, but I was moving like an out-of-shape desk jockey, my legs still totally wobbly. The heat was intense, making sweat pour down my face and back.

Maximus glanced back from up ahead, frowning at the sight of me lagging behind. He spun on a dime, racing back to me.

Without saying a word, he swooped me up into his arms and threw me over his shoulder.

"Oof." The air whooshed from my lungs as my stomach slammed into him.

"Hang on." He sprinted faster, and there was no doubt that I was moving quicker on his back.

How embarrassing.

"I can't hold it much longer." Prometheus panted.

Maximus ran faster, but the flames flickered and died a moment later. We kept running, though, so fast that the ground was a blur in front of my eyes as I bounced along on Maximus's back.

I heard the Echidna shriek from behind me, and lifted my head to look back. The three of them had appeared, perched on the rocks above. They looked entirely unharmed by the fire, and their eyes glowed bright with malice. They searched the area where we ran, their eyes racing over it. Almost as if they couldn't see me. Then their noses twitched.

"We're invisible," Prometheus whispered from where he ran along beside Maximus and me. "Illusion."

Ah, right. He was a trickster god, which probably brought with it the power of illusion.

"They can smell us," Maximus murmured.

I clung to Maximus, unable to look away from the Echidna, who were still scenting the air.

"I can run," I whispered at Maximus's back.

"Not fast enough."

Instead of throwing fire or sonic booms at us, the Echidna began to move, racing toward me. Their double tails moved gracefully on the rocks as they climbed over.

Oh no. "They're coming."

Within seconds, the Echidna were in front of us.

Oh fates, they're fast.

Dark delight lit their features, and they grinned evilly, white fangs glinting.

They raised their hands, magic sparking around their palms. Blue, green, red, they were ready to throw their entire arsenal toward us.

A glint of silvery water caught my eye.

There was a waterfall behind them, just to the left.

Heck yeah.

I called upon it with my magic, feeling the crisp bite of the water as it poured down the cliff face behind the Echidna. The water came easily to me—easier than it ever had before.

Quickly, it surged forward, a wide silver spear that plowed into the Echidna's backs. The snake women hissed in rage, plowing forward and slamming into the ground.

Maximus sprinted away, moving as fast as he could. Up ahead, I spotted the end of this narrow valley. We were almost to the end.

Prometheus pointed. "That's the boundary to their territory. We make it there, we're safe."

As soon as the words left his lips, a shiver ran down my spine.

Something was coming. I lifted my head to look, catching sight of the Echidna, who'd scrambled after us on their slithery bottom halves.

Man, they recovered quickly.

They darted toward a rock formation that was only a couple feet high, grabbing something in their hands. They lifted it, the three of them bearing the heavy weight of what looked like a tangled rope.

Then they threw it.

"Move!" I shouted to Maximus and Prometheus, but it was too late.

The net flew toward us, so fast I could hardly see it move. When the heavy weight landed on me and Maximus, my muscles froze solid. Maximus fell forward, and I went down right along with him, unable to move a muscle. I couldn't even move my eyeballs, though I was able to spot Prometheus going down with us. He was just as frozen as we were. When I hit the ground, my head slammed into a rock.

Blackness followed.

Pain streaked through my head as I woke from a deep sleep.

Sleep?

I couldn't be sleeping. I was upright, for one, tied to a chair with my head aching like I'd been hit with a truck. Agony radiated through my brain, and the muscles in my shoulders pulled.

It took everything I had to pry my eyes open. Sand seemed to scrape beneath my eyelids, burning my eyes.

A great fire roared in front of me, sending flickering shadows over the interior of a huge cave. Stalactites hung from the ceiling, piercing downward. A glance to my left and right showed Prometheus and Maximus in the same position.

How had we gotten here?

I tried to call upon my magic, but it stayed dormant inside me. The ropes had to be suppressing it somehow.

A memory of the snake women flashed in my mind.

Crap.

I blinked, searching the cave for them. When the red one slithered out from behind the fire, her dual tails carrying her quickly across the dirt ground, I winced backward.

There was only one way to describe the look in her eyes, and that was *hungry.*

Only then did I notice the weird iron bar that extended horizontally over the blazing fire.

"Oh fates, is that a *spit*?" I blurted the question, so horrified that I couldn't keep it in my mouth.

The red Echidna grinned evilly. "How else are we supposed to make dinner?"

There was no meat in the cave that I could see. So yeah, it was pretty obvious who was going to be dinner. Frantic, I struggled at the rope that wrapped around my chest and arms. My hands were bound behind me, which explained the pain in my shoulders. The ropes were so tight that I couldn't move an inch, and frustrated tears pricked at the corners of my eyes.

Maximus and Prometheus were now coming to, and the shock on their faces scared me even more. They were struggling to break their bindings, and they couldn't.

These were two men who were clearly used to muscling their way out of any situation they didn't like. And it wasn't working.

These were some seriously strong ropes.

I swallowed hard and turned back to the Echidna, struggling uselessly at my bonds. The knot was at the back—if there even was a knot—and there was no way for me to reach it.

The other two Echidna slithered out from behind the fire, their blue and green tails glinting like jewels in the light. The three of them slid toward me, eyes gleaming bright.

They ignored Maximus and Prometheus, leaning over to sniff me.

Surprise flared in their eyes, and they looked at each other.

"She smells of the ones on the mountain," whispered the blue-eyed one.

"Who are they?" I demanded.

The Echidna just stared at me, then slithered back toward the fire, leaning toward each other. They whispered frantically, and I called upon my gift from Artemis, using my animal hearing to pick up traces of their words.

"Should we eat her?"

"Will the gods be angry?"

"She's a trespasser."

"What about the winged ones?"

Who the hell were the winged ones?

The Echidna looked at me, calculation in their eyes. I glared back, and they turned away, resuming their conversation. They'd lowered their voices enough that I couldn't pick up on their words anymore, so I looked at Maximus and Prometheus. Both were red-faced as they struggled at their bonds.

Maximus was actually having some luck. The ropes were beginning to fray at his elbows, where he was shoving them away from his chest.

"Just a few minutes more," he murmured, so low I could barely hear.

My mind whirred. It'd definitely be a good thing if he could break free, but we all needed to escape at the same time if we wanted any hope of fighting off the Echidna. They'd go for us immediately, and we'd need all our skills to take them out.

Something small nudged my thigh, and I jumped.

I looked down, spotting Romeo's toothy grin. Poppy and Eloise stood by him.

Shit!

Then they disappeared.

"I've hidden them," Prometheus whispered.

Thank fates for illusion.

I'm working on your bindings. Romeo's voice sounded in my head. *Poppy is on the big stranger.*

"Where's Eloise?" I breathed. Maximus had it under control with his enormous gladiator strength.

Distraction.

Just then, a sound echoed from behind the fire. A rock falling.

The heads of the three Echidna whipped up, then they slithered behind the fire, searching for the source of the noise. It was all the time we needed.

My bindings fell loose, and so did Prometheus's. Maximus surged free as his ropes snapped, falling to the ground.

I sprinted toward the tall bonfire, using it as cover.

"We're invisible," Prometheus whispered. "And I've bought us a few moments." He hiked a thumb behind him, and I looked back.

My brows jumped.

In the three chairs sat myself, Maximus, and Prometheus, still bound.

"You're good," I murmured, so low even I could barely hear it.

Together, we crept around the flames, spying on the Echidna. They were at the back wall of the cave, searching the crevices in the rock for whatever had made the sound. They were like bloodhounds on the scent, determined to find what had disturbed their habitat.

We could run for it now, but they'd figure out we were gone before too long. And they were so fast they would definitely catch us. We needed to take them out while we had the chance.

I glanced up, spotting the stalactites on the ceiling. There were even more over here, and if we were lucky, they might be useful.

I pointed upward. "Let's knock them down."

I dug into my potion bag and withdrew one of the disintegration bombs. If I threw it just right, it could dislodge the stalactites without destroying the whole thing.

Romeo, tell Eloise to clear out, away from the back wall. No way I wanted my plan to squish my badger buddy.

Maximus drew his round shield from the ether, and Prometheus's hands lit up with fire.

All clear, Romeo said.

"Go," I whispered.

As one, we hurled our weapons. I chucked my potion bomb at the biggest stalactites, while Prometheus shot a blast of fire so strong it dislodged another one. Maximus hurled his shield, which flew through the air and slammed into the base of one of the protruding rocks.

As the three limestone spikes plummeted, I drew another potion bomb from my pack. Prometheus created another fireball, while Maximus caught his rebounding shield. One of the stalactites hit the red-headed Echidna right on the head. She collapsed.

The others shrieked their rage, their eyes frantically searching the cave for us. They glanced right over our forms, tricked my Prometheus's illusion.

The three of us threw our projectiles at the ceiling again, breaking away another series of stalactites. Then another. Within seconds, we'd knocked out all of the Echidna. They lay amongst the tumbled rocks, still as corpses.

Prometheus let his illusion magic fade, and suddenly I could see the Menacing Menagerie, standing near the fire. They crept toward the bodies of the Echidna.

"No way they're dead." Prometheus shook his head. "Too bad."

"Better that way," I said. "I'm supposed to prove myself by getting up this mountain, not kill all the citizens."

Even though they're jerks? Romeo asked.

"Yeah." I nodded, hurrying toward the Echidna to make sure they were well and truly out. "This is their turf. We were trespassing. They were just doing what monsters do."

Upon closer inspection, all of the Echidna were definitely out cold. Maximus conjured some iron shackles and bound their snake tails together.

Once he'd finished, he brushed off his hands and stood back.

"They'll get out of those eventually, but they should buy us enough time."

I grinned. "Good. Let's get a move on."

"This way." Prometheus waved his hand to indicate we should follow him, then led us out.

"You've been down here before?" I asked.

"Long ago. Before the Echidna even moved in."

We hurried away from the snake women and their fire, finding a huge tunnel that exited the cavern.

"What do you think she meant, that you smell like the ones on the mountain?" Maximus asked as we walked.

"I don't know. But she said something about the winged ones."

Maximus raised his brows. "Interesting."

"Seriously." My sisters had both gotten wings when they'd become Dragon Gods. To be honest, I'd quite like a pair myself.

Unless I turned into a bug. That'd be a letdown.

I grinned, and we continued on, following the scent of fresh air. The Menacing Menagerie hurried along beside me, their little feet moving fast on the dusty ground.

"I think we're nearly to the cave exit," I murmured.

We stepped out into the sunlight a moment later. The roar of a waterfall sounded to my left, and I looked over, spotting the falls that I'd used to knock over the Echidna. We were at the very end of their gauntlet.

"Let's hurry." Prometheus led us away from the valley, and we hurried up the mountain. The path narrowed as we climbed, falling away on either side. We could probably climb on the lower portion, but I didn't want to. The ground looked rocky and uneven.

A while later, we reached a part of the mountain where the ground flattened out. The peak rose high in the distance, still a long way off.

Prometheus led us toward the sound of water, and we reached a waterfall that flowed down a sharp cliff. I craned my neck, looking up. There was no easy way to ascend.

"Are you sure this is the right way?" I asked.

"Not entirely, no," Prometheus said. "This looks different than it did last time I was here. It's been a couple thousand years, though. The waterfall is new."

I frowned, inspecting the waterfall that flowed into a river at the base. The wide rush of water flowed across the flat plain upon which we stood, then poured down the mountain in the distance. The cliff wall on either side of the falls was perfectly smooth. Terrible for climbing.

I moved closer to the falls, my ears picking up the sound of rustling in the grass that surrounded the river. The Menacing Menagerie stopped abruptly, their eyes glued to the grass.

Visitor. Romeo looked at me.

"What kind?"

Don't know.

A moment later, a small cat with russet fur crept out. Some kind of wildcat with bright yellow eyes and an intelligent face.

"Hello," I said.

"Not sure he can talk back," Prometheus said.

"I wouldn't be so sure." Romeo had shocked the hell out of me when he'd started talking. And I had Artemis's gift of an affinity for animals. There was no telling what this wildcat might be able to communicate.

For now, though, she just stared at me suspiciously.

"We're trying to get to the top of Olympus. Any advice?" I asked.

The cat tilted her head, as if she could understand me. I called upon Artemis's magic, trying to forge a connection with the little feline.

Almost immediately, I felt her life force. Her eyes widened, almost as if understanding dawned upon her.

Suddenly, a thought blasted into my mind.

We needed to climb up the cliff, right behind the waterfall. There was a passage there that would lead us higher into the mountain. The cat never took that path—never went any higher on the mountain, in fact—but she'd heard of it.

"Thanks," I said.

The cat inclined its head, then trotted off, slipping into the bushes once more.

I turned to Maximus and Prometheus, who were looking at me like I was nuts. They hadn't heard my communication with the cat—even I hadn't really *heard* it so much as felt it. "We have to climb up behind the waterfall. There's a tunnel back there that will lead us farther up."

"The cat told you that?" Doubt echoed in Prometheus's voice.

"Yep."

He shrugged. "Fine enough. Makes sense. The waterfall was likely diverted this way after my last visit. I think I recall climbing a cliff."

I gave him a skeptical look. He was good as far as guides went—he'd gotten us all this way—but I wouldn't be five-starring him on Trip Advisor. Four point five stars, max.

We skirted around the edge of the river, going right up to the base of the waterfall. The river poured down, speckling my face with droplets. I edged up to the side of the falls and peered behind. The water arced away from the cliff, forming a pocket within which we could climb.

I spotted several indented handholds in the rock and grinned. "Jackpot."

I glanced down at the Menacing Menagerie. Romeo was frowning at the rock face.

"See you later?" I asked.

Yep.

With that, the Menagerie disappeared.

"Let's go." I jumped on the wet rocks that lined the area behind the falls, making my way toward the middle where the handholds were etched into the rock.

Maximus and Prometheus followed, silent and quick.

I began to climb, finding the handholds easily. There wasn't much light back here, but it was enough to illuminate the grips. The stone was wet beneath my fingertips, but rough enough that I had a good handhold.

Water roared behind me as I climbed, water droplets splashing the backs of my jeans. Probably my jacket, too, but I couldn't feel it through the leather.

I was nearly to the top when I gripped the handhold that was actually a huge hole in the cliff wall. It was the tunnel that the wildcat had mentioned.

I scrambled up into it, climbing to my feet in the dark space. Maximus and Prometheus followed. I shook my hand, igniting the magic in my lightstone ring. It flared to life, sending a golden glow over the huge cavern.

Prometheus stepped forward. "Yes, this is familiar."

"Any monsters in here?" Maximus asked.

Prometheus shrugged. "Probably. But they'll likely be different than when I was here last."

Just our luck.

We started through the tunnel, which was at least thirty feet across. It sloped gradually upward as we travelled, extending through the mountainside.

After about half an hour, we reached a wider cavern. It was huge, soaring at least a hundred feet overhead.

Aaaand...it was a dead end.

I stopped abruptly. "Well, shit."

6

Strangely, the enormous cavern was filled with fallen trees. Their roots protruded upward from the ends, grasping like claws. The wood was bleached by age, making the trees look more like giant bones.

"How could a forest grow underground?" Maximus asked. "This must have once been on the surface."

Prometheus nodded. "I believe so. Something has reshaped this part of the mountain."

"But why?" I asked.

Prometheus shrugged. "War? Building a home? Your guess is as good as mine."

Prometheus pointed upward toward the ceiling on the far side of the cavern. "I think there may be an exit over there."

I squinted toward it, spotting a thick layer of vines twisting over the cavern wall.

"There's an exit behind the vines," Prometheus said. "I remember climbing the cliff behind the waterfall—though there was no waterfall at the time—and then ascending another cliff. I think this cavern is part of that."

"Let's try it, then." Maximus strode toward one of the massive fallen trees and bent over to pick it up. The thing was at least three feet in diameter and had to weigh thousands of pounds, but he didn't so much as break a sweat.

He swung it around and lifted one end high, then propped it against the far wall like a slanted ladder. He looked back at Prometheus. "How's this?"

"Move the top end a little to the left."

Maximus did as requested.

"Good enough." Prometheus strode toward the log ladder and began to climb, moving nimbly toward the top.

I waited at the bottom, watching. Maximus joined me.

Prometheus reached the vines that covered the wall and pressed his hands to them. He waited a moment, then turned back to us. "I think this is it. I feel a slight draft."

"Should we come up?" I shouted.

"Let me blast these away first." Fire glowed orange around his hands, and he shot it toward the vine.

Instead of burning and withering away, they absorbed the fire, growing thicker.

Prometheus cursed. "Second time my fire has backfired." He looked back at us, a sour twist to his mouth. "No pun intended."

"I can try something." I stepped forward.

"Good." He sprinted back down the log. "Because I need to come up with some new tricks."

Maybe. But with illusion magic like his, he was still loaded for bear.

I traded spots with him on the log and hurried to the top, feeling like a gymnast—a very unskilled one—on a balance beam. I reached the vines and eyed them warily. They were thick and green, looking like they might want to reach out and grab me.

I raised a hand and pressed it to the smooth surface that was as wide around as a two-liter Coke bottle. Immediately, I felt the strength in the vine.

Whoa.

This thing was strong. It fairly pulsed with life. I closed my eyes and called on my death magic, sucking the life from the vine. It flowed up my arm and into my soul, filling me with immense energy.

Once the transfer started, I opened my eyes. The vine withered in front of my face, shrinking away to nothing. I touched another vine, drawing out more energy. I kept going until I'd revealed a tunnel and my limbs vibrated with power. I was so full of it that I felt like I could jump to the moon.

I turned back to the guys. "We're in."

Maximus and Prometheus approached the log. I looked back at the tunnel, which was entirely dark, and entered.

The air smelled wetter here, almost alive. I raised my lightstone ring and shined the golden glow on the tunnel's interior.

Dozens of eyes stared back, and I stifled a scream, lunging backward. Strong hands gripped my back, stopping me from going any farther.

"Oh, fates." Maximus sounded horrified.

I blinked once at the enormous spider-like monsters that stared at us. No, not spiders. Scorpions.

And they were huge.

Giant stinger tails and pincers—even fangs that dripped with green venom.

They lunged, so fast that I almost missed the movement. My heart leapt into my throat, nearly choking me.

Instinct drove me. I called on the magic that I'd just absorbed, flinging it outward at the scorpions. The power sizzled as it left my fingertips, hot and bright. It exploded out of me as a flame, driving the scorpions back.

Prometheus joined me, throwing his own fire at the

monsters. He grinned as they scuttled backward, avoiding the blast of our flames.

"Pretty handy now." He glanced at me. "I didn't know you could control fire."

"Neither did I." I watched the stuff bursting from my finger-tips. "I think I got it from you."

His brows jumped. "Well, I certainly didn't *give* it to you."

"No, I think it came from the vine." It had absorbed his magic, and when I'd sucked the life out of the plant, the magic had come with it. Just another way the death magic was changing within me—and remaining my most useful power. "Let's move forward. Maybe we can sneak past the scorpions."

I'd kill them if there was no other choice. But I didn't want to if I didn't have to. Once again, this was just a case of monsters being monsters.

Prometheus and I took the front, while Maximus took the back, drawing his shield and sword to protect our flanks. Slowly, we moved through the tunnel, keeping the flames blasting in front of us.

The scorpions continued to scuttle away, hissing and thrusting their spiked tails at us. As we got deeper into the tunnel, one snuck around the side and attempted to strike from the back.

My stomach dropped. Maximus lunged, and I heard him more than saw him. A scorpion hissed loudly, and I glanced backward.

Maximus had severed one claw, and the scorpion was glaring at him.

"There's more where that came from," Maximus said.

I chuckled at the dad joke.

The scorpion seemed to get the gist and stayed back. We made our way through the tunnel, finally reaching a spot where it diverged into two.

"Right or left?" I asked Prometheus.

He squinted at both, clearly debating. "Let's try right."

He didn't sound very confident. "Still looks different than last time you were here?"

"Yeah. But it feels like the right one."

"Good enough for me." I moved toward it, directing my fire to keep the scorpions to the left.

They scuttled out of the way, and we hurried into the second tunnel.

"There aren't any in this one." Prometheus killed his flame and turned to face backward. He lit up again, blasting the fire back at the scorpions.

I mimicked his movements, and we kept it up until we were out of harm's way.

"I think we're good," Prometheus said.

"I'll hear them if they try to approach."

We killed the flame and Maximus stowed his weapons, then we continued on through the tunnel. Our footsteps were silent, and I heard no other sounds but the slight huff of our breaths.

Gradually, the slope of the tunnel ascended, and the air began to smell of cooking meat.

I sniffed deeply. "Man, that smells good."

"Who would be cooking down here?" Maximus asked.

"There are a few options," Prometheus said. "Most of whom we probably don't want to meet."

"Let's take a diverging path if we find one." I raised my light-stone ring higher, hoping to see another split in the path.

I didn't, and the route we were on led into another enormous cavern. Huge rock formations filled the space, and it took me a moment to realize that they kind of looked like furniture.

"Oh fates," I murmured.

"Giants," Maximus whispered.

I looked at Prometheus, whose brow was creased with worry. "Let's move quickly. Quietly. Keep to the shadows."

I gestured for him to lead the way, and he did. We skirted around the side of the cave at first. I spotted no one. Halfway through the cavern, we darted to the middle, where we could hide beneath the massive table.

Once again, I felt like a mouse. Sneaking up on the giant Titans had been hard enough. This was extra freaky since I didn't know exactly what was coming.

Fortunately, the cavern remained empty. Whoever lived here was gone.

We hurried to the edge of the table and peeked out into the open cavern. There was a stone couch covered in massive cushions about forty yards away.

Prometheus pointed to it, and I nodded. As a group, we sprinted toward it, then slipped underneath. Whoever had built it was so big that the space under the couch was five feet high. I could nearly stand upright.

We moved quickly through the shadows and headed for the other side.

When the ground began to vibrate slightly beneath my feet, I stiffened.

Prometheus and Maximus did the same, each turning to look at me.

"Company," I whispered.

We snuck to the edge of the couch, and I peered out just in time to see an enormous Cyclops enter the room. He was huge —at least forty feet tall—and his one eye was a brilliant blue. An animal hide was draped over his shoulder, and he carried a club in one hand.

Oh man, he looked strong.

I shrank back into the shadows of the couch.

"Who's there?" the Cyclops bellowed. His voice was so deep

and scratchy it sounded like he was speaking through a throat full of gravel.

I froze, my heart thundering. Had he heard me?

"I can smell you, intruders."

Crap!

I had no way to make myself not smell like a human. I met Maximus and Prometheus's gazes, but before we could even whisper a plan, there was a loud thud.

I whirled toward the noise, spotting the face of the Cyclops pressed right against the ground. He glared at me with his one eye, then reached under the couch and wrapped a meaty hand around my waist. He moved so fast I didn't have a chance to run.

He yanked me out from under the couch, and my skin chilled. Then he reached down with his other hand and grabbed someone else.

Maximus.

Damn.

He stood, raising us into the air. My head swam as the earth rushed away from me, and I tried to gasp in a breath.

"There's another one," the Cyclops said.

Oh, crap. Who was he talking to?

I peered around to the side, spotting a second Cyclops. He was just as big as his buddy, but with blond hair instead of brown. He bent down and snatched up Prometheus.

Dang it.

There went our backup.

I dragged in a ragged breath, barely able to fill my lungs with how hard the Cyclops was gripping me. "Lighten up."

He just glared at me.

I called upon my magic, debating which power to use. Should I suck the life from him? There was probably so much inside him that I'd explode from it. I could try the sunlight power to blind him, or the lightning.

"Don't attack!" Prometheus gasped.

Did he mean *me*?

I twisted my neck to look at him.

Overhead, the Cyclops said, "I should hope not. Guests in my home, attacking?"

Guests?

I shot a quizzical look at Prometheus, and he repeated the command. "Don't attack." He turned to look up at the Cyclops. "But could you loosen your grip, please?"

What the heck was going on?

The grip around my chest loosened, though, just enough to let me breathe freely. I sucked in a deep breath and looked up at the Cyclops. He was looking down at me with confusion, but not menace.

Okay, *were* we guests here?

The truth was, we were intruders. But maybe he could see past that. Prometheus seemed to know something was up.

"Hi," I said.

"Arges, Steropes, it's good to see you," Prometheus said. "I didn't realize you lived here, now."

The Cyclops holding me looked between me and Prometheus. He squinted toward Prometheus, then grinned widely, his teeth yellowed and chipped. He had to be thousands of years old, and he definitely needed a trip to the dentist.

"Prometheus!" he boomed. "It's been a long time. You look quite different."

Prometheus rubbed a hand over his smooth chin. "No more beard."

The Cyclops nodded, then stomped toward the big table in the middle. I bounced in his hand with every step, and managed to catch Maximus's eye. The corner of his mouth quirked up.

The Cyclops set me on the table, along with Maximus. The one holding Prometheus did the same.

Prometheus stepped forward, gesturing to me and Maximus. "I'd like to introduce you to my friends. This is Maximus Valerius, the gladiator, and this is Rowan Blackwood, the Greek Dragon God."

The Cyclopes each sat heavily in a stone chair and nodded at us.

The one who had been holding me said, "I am Arges."

"And I am Steropes," said the other. He turned to look at Prometheus. "What are you doing in our home, sneaking around?"

Prometheus grinned, and I was grateful to see that he didn't look very nervous. Which was good, since I was plenty nervous. These guys seemed nice, but they were still big enough to eat me in one bite.

"Well, we didn't realize it was your home. You lived in mountains farther west when I knew you last. And we were sneaking because we needed to pass through, but we didn't know that friends lived here."

Steropes nodded. "We came here two thousand years ago and built this place."

Prometheus nodded. "I noticed the changes."

Ah, so these were the ones who'd diverted the river and built the caves.

"There was nothing big enough, or safe enough, for us." Arges swept his hand around the room. "But now we have this place."

"Where is Brontes?" Prometheus asked.

I looked at him, confused, and he silently mouthed, "Third Cyclops."

There were *three*? Fantastic.

"Off foraging," Steropes said. "But we have some nice wild boar roasting in the other room."

So that was the smell of cooking meat I'd gotten a whiff of.

My stomach grumbled.

The Cyclops grinned down at me. "Hungry, human?"

"Oh, I'm fine."

He glowered, and I winced.

"Of course she's hungry!" Prometheus smiled widely. "Just not used to Cyclopian manners." He glared at me. "I, too, am famished."

I nodded quickly. "What he said."

The Cyclops stopped glowering and stood, slapping his hands on his knees. "Good. Then I will be right back."

The two Cyclopes left the room, and Prometheus turned to me. "*Always* accept a Cyclops's hospitality."

"Gotcha." A thought occurred. "It won't be poisonous, right? And if we eat it, we won't be forced to stay here?"

"That rule only applies to Hades."

"You've known these Cyclopes for years?" Maximus asked.

"Many years. And even better, we parted on good terms." He grinned. "I'm about to prove very useful."

"You stopped me from getting eaten, so yeah, I'd say you've proven your worth."

The sound of stomping footsteps returned, and the Cyclopes entered, each carrying a tray of glistening meat. The haunches of boar were enormous. Far bigger than any animal I'd ever seen.

Maximus and I scrambled out of the way as they slammed the platters down onto the table. The boar was taller than I was.

"Olympian boar." Arges smiled widely.

Prometheus walked toward the huge tower of meat, grabbed a piece with his bare hand, and tore the flesh away.

I wasn't super picky about manners, but grabbing a handful of boar meat was outside of my usual, to be honest. But I mimicked his gesture, grabbing my own handful of steaming boar.

The first bite was divine, and I got over my squeamishness quickly. I figured it was best to follow Prometheus's lead in this, so I ate until he stopped. Maximus did the same.

Finally, when everyone was sated, Arges sat back and looked at us. "You never answered why you were here."

"I have to get to the top of the mountain," I said. "Three of the Titans have escaped Tartarus, and if we want to put them back there, I need to complete my transition to Dragon God."

Both of the Cyclopes scowled. "The Titans?"

"You know them?"

As soon as the words left my mouth, I realized it was a dumb question. I'd read something about the Titans and Cyclopes a while ago. There was so much to Greek myth that it was sometimes hard to keep it all straight, but they didn't like each other, as I recalled.

"Of course we knew them!" Arges bellowed. "Those bastards kept us chained up in Tartarus for millennia."

"Only Zeus saw fit to free us," Steropes said. "So now we protect him."

That sounded fair.

"Will you help us stop them, then?" I asked. "Help us get to the top of Olympus. Please."

Both Cyclopes pursed their lips, clearly thinking.

"Yes, we can do that," Arges said. "And if you ever need help on the field of battle, we would like to be there."

Steropes cracked his knuckles and grinned. "It would be an honor."

"Nay, a pleasure," Arges said.

I smiled back. "Excellent. We could use all the help we can get."

"Good. It is decided." Steropes nodded. "We will take you to the top of the mountain now."

A smile split across my face. "Thank you."

They both stood, surging to their feet in one swift motion.

Arges gripped me around the waist and set me on his shoulder, then put Maximus next to me. I crouched down and gripped the animal skin tunic that stretched over his shoulder. Maximus knelt next to me, grabbing on as well.

Once Prometheus was settled on Steropes's shoulder, the giants took off, striding through their cavern and down a massive tunnel. The air smelled damp but relatively clean, and the Cyclopes obviously took very good care of their underground lair. Not what I'd expected, but I was grateful.

When they strode out into the sunlight, I took a deep breath. *Onward.*

7

The Cyclopes climbed up the mountain, which seemed to have tripled in size. The boulders were bigger, and so were the cliffs. It would have been an enormous endeavor without their help.

The cool breeze blew the hair back from my face as we ascended. The air grew colder, and I shivered and retreated into my jacket.

Maximus's magic flared on the air, and a warm hat and gloves appeared in his hands. "Here."

I took them, smiling gratefully, and put them on. "Ahhh. That's awesome."

"Glad to be of service."

I bumped my shoulder against his just to feel him, then looked over at Prometheus. He looked a bit pale as we climbed higher, and I remembered that we were approaching Zeus's domain. Prometheus probably didn't want to see the guy, given their history.

I leaned up toward Arges's ear. "Are you taking us right to Zeus's place?"

"To the base. We won't approach his castle, but we'll get you as close as we can."

"Thanks." I looked over at Prometheus. "Since we're nearly there, you can bail whenever."

He glanced at me. "Oh, I plan to."

We rode higher, jostling along. Snow began to fall, and there was a thick accumulation of it on the ground. We were so high up that the air was thin and cold.

"Winter sucks on Olympus," Prometheus muttered. "The poets never speak of that."

I wouldn't say that it sucked—it was really quite beautiful, with the sparkling white stuff covering the huge trees and boulders—but it was cold. My breath began to puff out as little white clouds.

"Nearly there," Arges said.

We had almost reached the clouds, and when we entered them, the air was cold and damp. I could barely see more than ten feet in front of my face.

A moment later, we broke through the cloud layer, arising into the bright sunlight. It gleamed off the golden marble castle that crouched on the mountaintop several hundred feet above us.

"That is Zeus's domain." Arges pointed at it, then moved his finger to indicate a lower level. "And that is where I am taking you."

I dragged my gaze from the golden castle and spotted the white settlement down below. It didn't appear as if anyone lived there, but the white marble columns and platforms made it look like some kind of strange ceremonial center.

Arges climbed right to it, then took us down from his shoulder and set us in the middle of the space below the castle. It was about the size of a football field, with massive columns all around. Six large platforms made of more white marble were situated in a circle around an open area in the middle.

Steropes deposed Prometheus and set him next to us. "Goodbye, new friends, and best of luck."

With that, the Cyclopes disappeared down the mountainside.

Prometheus shivered and glared around the place, eventually turning his gaze up toward Zeus's castle, which sat on the rocks about a hundred feet above. His scowl deepened, and when I followed his gaze, I spotted an enormous man standing on the ramparts of the castle.

The man's beard and long, flowing hair were as white as the marble upon which he stood. Even from this distance, I could see his blue eyes blazing down at us. In his hand, he gripped a crooked golden rod, and I realized it was shaped like a lightning bolt.

Awe filtered through me. "Zeus."

I didn't like a lot of the things Zeus had done, but he was still the most powerful Greek god in existence. It was hard not to be a little awed by the magnitude of his power, even as I disagreed with how he used it.

"The bastard himself." Prometheus turned to us. "Well, I've fulfilled my side of the bargain. You're here. Try not to die."

A grin tugged at the corner of my mouth. "That's at the top of my to-do list every day."

Maximus inclined his head in a goodbye.

Prometheus turned back to Zeus and flipped him the bird, waving his hand around so the god was sure to see the middle finger. He grinned widely as he did it, then glanced at me. "This is half the reason I came this far."

Oh fates, he's going to piss off the most powerful god there is!

Before Zeus could retaliate, Prometheus moved his hand in a

large circle, creating the same terrifyingly windy portal that he'd made back in Istanbul. Without hesitating, he stepped into it and was gone.

Warily, I glanced up at Zeus, who was scowling at the empty space Prometheus had left behind. He didn't seem to be about to throw a lightning bolt at us, so my shoulders relaxed.

I turned to inspect the space upon which we stood. "I wonder if we should go up to the castle?"

"I have no idea." Maximus frowned up at Zeus. "He doesn't look particularly welcoming."

"But he's not firing lightning bolts at us, so I'll take that as a good thing."

Maximus wrapped an arm around my shoulders and tugged me to him in a quick hug. "I like how you think."

"This place feels powerful, doesn't it?" I could feel the magic vibrating through my body, and I was pretty sure it wasn't all coming from Zeus. "It feels as if it's imbued with ancient magic."

"It does." Maximus released my shoulders and strode into the middle of the space. "There's definitely something special here."

I followed him, entering the open area that sat in the middle of the large stone platforms. Each looked like they were big enough to hold a rock band.

"This has to be something ceremonial." Was I supposed to do something here? At this point, I was pretty much out of ideas.

A shriek sounded from above, and I jumped, nearly coming out of my skin. Heart pounding, I looked upward.

A massive bird flew in the pure blue sky. It had wings so big that I could barely conceive of it.

"Holy fates." I staggered backward. "That's not a bird."

"It's a dragon." Awe echoed in Maximus's voice.

I blinked up at the massive creature, barely able to process it. Dragons were incredibly rare creatures. The only one that I'd ever seen was Ladon, the Greek dragon I'd met in the Garden of the Hesperides, and Arach, the dragon spirit who presided over the Protectorate castle. Arach was usually in her ghostly human form, though, so that didn't quite count.

This dragon had glittering black scales and enormous wings. Its long neck was graceful and its tail powerful. Spikes protruded from its back, each streaked through with red.

"That looks like Ladon," I said.

"It does." Maximus pointed right. "There's another."

I looked over, joy jumping in my chest as I saw another dragon. This one was bigger and stockier, with a wider body and a much shorter neck. The scales were a brilliant green, and the horns were enormous. "It's a totally different kind of dragon."

"That one, too." Maximus pointed again, and I followed the gesture, spotting a red dragon.

Movement to the right caught my eye. "And another!"

This one was blue. Within seconds, we saw two more. The six of them circled the sky, flying overhead.

"I think they're checking us out," Maximus said.

Delight warred with fear inside my body. Dragons were an unknown. Ladon had helped us once, but would these dragons? Or would they want to eat us?

A tiny part of me wanted to run and hide—heck, I was no moron—but it was a terrible idea. We needed to stand our ground.

Actually, maybe only I needed to stand my ground. I didn't want to risk Maximus's life on my hunch. "Go hide."

His head swiveled on his neck, and he shot me an incredulous look. "You're going to stand out here, and you expect me to go hide?"

"Fine." I realized what a dumb idea it was. With him giving me that look, it was hard not to. "I just wanted to protect you."

His expression softened. "I know. But I'm not hiding while

you wait to meet a bunch of dragons. One, I want to meet them, too. And two, if they decide to eat you, I'm not going to watch from a hiding place."

"Good point." I smiled at him, glad to have him at my back.

He grinned, and the feeling that bloomed in my chest was so warm and bright that it felt like my heart was turning into the sun and rising. I gasped, stunned by the feeling.

The dragons shrieked again, all six in unison, and my gaze was dragged upward.

They descended gracefully toward the ground, flying in a clockwise circle as they approached. One by one, each landed on a stone platform.

Awed, I spun in a circle to take them all in. Their magic rolled over me in an intense wave, making me feel lightheaded and powerful all at the same time.

They were all remarkably different up close, each a different species. Perhaps even a different culture. The blue one looked a lot like a Chinese dragon from illustrations that I'd seen, while the red one looked like the dragon that decorated the Welsh flag. There was also a gold dragon, a green one with three heads, and one that appeared to be made of ice. Since Ladon was definitely the Greek dragon, these ones must've been from other places.

I'm meeting the Council of Dragons.

I didn't know if that was what they formally called themselves, but that was what they appeared to be.

I turned toward Ladon, since he was the only one I knew. I drifted my hand toward my pocket, where I still kept the magical scale he'd given me. It turned into a boat upon command, and it was still one of the best gifts I'd ever received.

Instinct made me bow low, and Maximus did the same. I stayed that way for a few moments, then rose.

"Hello, Ladon." I spun in a circle again, my gaze landing on each dragon in turn. "Hello."

I wished I had something cleverer to say, but apparently six enormous dragons were enough to strike one dumb.

"Rowan Blackwood. Dragon God." Before, the dragon had spoken in my mind. This time, he spoke out loud. Was it the magic of Olympus that made that possible? Ladon turned his clever gaze to Maximus. "Maximus Valerius, gladiator."

"I was sent to you by the Great One of the Amazons," I said.

"Yes, we've been waiting." Ladon gestured to the dragon nearest him, the one who looked like he could lead a Chinese New Year's parade. "This is Lóng, my Chinese compatriot."

Ladon went around the circle, introducing me to the golden Indian dragon named Nāga, the green Slavic dragon named Zmiy, the red Welsh dragon named Y Ddraig Goch, and an Arctic dragon named Siku. Each nodded at me in turn, and the enormity of the situation made it nearly impossible for me to do anything more than nod in response.

It felt like my insides were full of butterflies—so many that I might lift off into the air at any moment.

"You are here to complete your transformation into a Dragon God so that you may defeat the Titans," Ladon said.

I nodded. "Complete my transformation into what?"

Please say dragon. Oh fates, I was about to pass out from excitement. If he said dragon, I probably would.

"That is yet to be determined," Ladon said.

Dang. But that didn't mean *no* dragon.

"What must I do?" I asked.

"I have seen you and believe in your strength." Ladon gestured to his companions. "But they have not. You must go on a journey to prove yourself."

I nodded. "Anything."

"You must go to the forest where Medusa dwells and return with her heads. You will find her by following the whistle."

Crap. Medusa? She was the dangerous one who turned

people to stone. That was going to be tough. I glanced at Maximus, and he looked concerned as well.

"Is there anything else I need to do?" I asked.

Ladon shook his head. "Do it quickly. And here." He climbed down off of his platform, his massive body graceful despite its bulk. He walked toward me, then handed me a sharp, curved object.

"A dragon's claw." Awe shot through me. The claw was about six inches long and gleamed like opals. I looked over toward Siku, the Arctic dragon. The claw matched the ones that tipped her toes, and she inclined her head.

"It will help you with Medusa," she said.

Was I supposed to stab her with it?

"Go now. And be quick." Ladon's words dragged me away from my question, and before I could voice it, the ether sucked me in and spun me through space.

When it spat me out in a shady forest, I gasped and stumbled, barely managing to keep my feet. Maximus appeared next to me.

"Did you get all of that?" I asked him.

He nodded. "But there was something strange that he said. We are supposed to retrieve Medusa's heads. Plural. But she only has one head."

"He didn't speak out loud before, in the Garden of the Hesperides. Maybe he's not used to it."

Maximus frowned. "Perhaps."

The forest shifted around us, the trees almost seeming to move. I stiffened, going on the alert, and spun in a circle to inspect our surroundings. Massive white trees surrounded us in the woods, their branches devoid of leaves. The forest floor was clear of underbrush, and the whole place vibrated with magic.

"She must live in this forest," I said.

"Hiding, perhaps."

I tilted my head, listening for the whistle that Ladon had mentioned. After a moment, I heard it, faintly. I pointed in the proper direction. "I hear the whistle from over there."

"So do I."

"We'll need a mirror to defeat her," I said. "We can't look directly upon her, but if we see her through a mirror, we may be all right."

Maximus nodded, conjuring two mirrors in plastic frames. "Since we don't know where she'll be, we should navigate using the mirror."

"Good plan." I didn't like the idea of becoming a statue by mistake because I unintentionally looked at her when she stepped out from behind a tree. If I did something that dumb, I'd probably end up in a museum with a sign that said *Statue of a Moron*.

I took the mirror from Maximus and held it so it showed the forest in front of me. It was a crappy way to travel, but if I used my animal hearing, it'd give me an advantage.

"Let's go," Maximus said.

As we crept through the woods, my heart started to pound in my chest. Looking through the mirror majorly upped the tension. The tiny window made it hard to see, and enemies could be lurking anywhere. Medusa might not be a giant monster with claws and fangs, but she was more dangerous. One mistaken look and...*done.*

Fear shivered over my spine. Would I be conscious if I were still a statue, trapped inside the stone forever?

Oh fates, that sounded awful.

In fact, it sounded a lot like my time in captivity with the Rebel Gods. I'd been under a spell most of the time. Sometimes I'd been totally unaware of my environment and actions, but other times I'd been trapped in my body, dreadfully aware of what was going on but unable to do anything to stop it.

The spells had made me the perfect captive and perfect tool for their evil deeds. But they'd also made me so miserable that I'd almost gone insane.

Medusa could do that to me.

A nightmare come true.

Fighting and killing one monster didn't sound that hard. But *Medusa*?

She was the worst monster of them all—at least for me.

I tried to shake away my fear and focus on the forest around me. We made slow progress through the trees, using the mirrors to guide us as we followed the faint whistling sound. My hearing picked up no sense of life around us. Not even the noise of wind through the trees.

"This place is eerie," Maximus whispered.

"I've no idea where we are." The forest felt like it was so far from civilization that it might as well have been on the moon. Why would Medusa choose to live here?

The thought was my last.

Something gripped me around my ankle and yanked me upward. My stomach lurched into my throat, and panic tightened my chest.

Oh shit!

I spun in the air, the world upside down.

"Hang on. I've got you." Maximus moved fast, conjuring a sword and slicing through the rope that suspended me.

I plummeted, and he caught me then spun me upright.

"What the hell was that?" I looked up, spotting the snare. "A booby trap?"

Maximus nodded. "We need to get out of here before the hunter comes."

I nodded. There might be no hunter—maybe we were

supposed to dangle there till we died—but I didn't want to wait and find out.

"Hang on." Maximus's magic flared, and he handed me a stick with a heavy wheel on the end. "Roll that in front of you. Hopefully it will trigger the snare if there are any more."

Man, he was clever. "Thanks."

He conjured one for himself, and we got the heck out of there, each of us navigating by mirror and rolling the sticks in front of us. It was a weird, slow way to travel, but it worked.

I kept my ears perked as we walked, hoping to hear the sound of the hunter coming to find us after the snare had been triggered. Maybe it was Medusa, trying to catch her prey.

My rolly-stick caught on two more snares as I walked, and each time, my heart jumped into my chest. Maximus also caught two snares, but after a while, they seemed to clear out.

Part of me was tempted to stop with the rolly-stick, but that was probably a bad idea. We kept going, moving as quickly as we could through the trees.

Eventually, we reached an area where massive twiggy bushes sat in the forest. Like the trees, they were devoid of leaves, but their branches were thick and strong. We stepped between two, and magic flared in the air.

I had barely a moment to process what was happening before sharp pain pierced my arms and legs. "Watch out!"

But it was too late. Thorns were flying at me from the bushes, striking my jacket and jeans like bullets, piercing my skin and sending pain through me.

Maximus grunted.

He was being hit, too.

We dropped to the ground, huddling together, and he conjured two massive shields that we used to cover ourselves. The thorns continued to fly, pinging off the shield.

Agony streaked through me from the thorns that had pierced me, and my head began to grow woozy.

"Poison." Maximus's voice was rough with pain.

Poison.

He was right. I could feel it streaking through me, weakening me with every second.

8

Maximus and I lay on the ground, our faces so close together that I could see the lines of agony cut around his eyes. Tiny thorns protruded from his clothes, the points stuck into his skin.

He should be immune to most injuries—a gift from the god who'd given him his magic. But this poison, whatever it was, seemed to be affecting him, too.

Pain streaked through my body, and my mind began to move slower as I tried to figure a way out of this. The thorns continued to ping against our shield, but our real problem was the poison in our veins.

I needed an antidote.

Shaking, I reached for the little vials in my potion belt. I gripped a general antidote and thrust it at Maximus. "Take this."

"You first."

"I've got another." I shoved it into his hand and reached for my belt again to withdraw a second. I had no idea if it would work against this poison, but it was my best shot.

I let go of the shield so it was propped against my back to protect me, then fumbled with the vial. I slugged it back, wincing at the sour taste. Maximus did the same, and I waited, praying.

Finally, some of the wooziness began to retreat from my mind. Strength returned to my limbs, and the tremors ceased.

"It's working," Maximus said.

"Thank fates."

"What is it?"

"General antidote, but an extra strong dose. I have a few like it, meant for different things. Some turn back the effects of poison, others break a strong spell. But since I invented them and haven't been able to test them in all circumstances, I'm never quite sure if they'll work when I need them to do something new."

Maximus grinned and pressed a quick kiss to my lips. "You're a genius."

I grinned, then winced at the pain that still sliced through the areas where the thorns stuck into my body. "We need to get these thorns out."

Maximus began to pluck the thorns out of my arms.

"Work on yourself," I said.

"You first."

Oh fates, this guy. I was totally falling for him. Had fallen, really. There was no question about it. Love.

I looked up at him, about to say something, when he grinned.

"Hear that?" he asked.

"What?"

"The thorns have stopped hitting us."

Oh, thank fates. The coast was clear.

Maybe.

"Did they stop because the bushes ran out of thorns, or because *someone* stopped them?"

"Good point." Maximus grabbed his mirror and surged to his

feet, protecting himself with the shield as he looked into the mirror and spun in a circle, checking our surroundings. "Coast is clear."

My shoulders relaxed just slightly. I stood and began to pluck the thorns out of my body. Maximus worked on himself, and soon we were thornless.

"There sure are a lot of booby traps in this forest," I said.

"It's odd, all right." He set off again, heading in the direction we'd been going, following the faint whistling noise that never let up.

We went as quickly as we could with the mirror, roll-stick, and shield, but it wasn't fast going. By the time I heard the rustling in the woods, I nearly jumped out of my skin.

When I spotted the Centaur behind me, my heart thundered. He was massive, at least eight feet tall with a powerful brown horse's body and a broad chest. A wound striped over his chest, yellow and green. Infected.

He raised a bow and arrow, sighted it at us.

Since he wasn't Medusa, I turned and looked at him straight on, holding up my hands. "Wait! We aren't here to hurt you."

He scowled, his dark brows crouching low over his eyes. "Then why are you here?"

"We're hunting Medusa."

His scowl deepened, and he drew back on the bow.

Well, shit, he didn't like the sound of that. My mind raced, trying to find something—anything—that would make him lower the bow. I could duck behind my shield, but I didn't want to start a fight with a guy who could outrun me and kick me in the head with his hooves.

"She can heal your wound," Maximus said.

I brightened. That was good.

The Centaur scowled. "I'm fine."

"You're not. It's infected." And he was a smart-seeming guy, so he'd probably tried to treat it. The fact that it was oozing yellow and green stuff made it likely the treatments hadn't been working. "I'm a potion master. I'm sure I have something to fix that."

The Centaur scowled again and didn't lower his bow.

"Please, let me help you," I said.

He glared at us, clearly considering. Then he nodded. "Fine."

My shoulders relaxed. Okay. This was good. I could work with this. Just like the mouse that had pulled the thorn out of the lion's foot, I would help this guy.

Slowly, I approached him. His bow stayed lowered, thank fates. Maximus stuck close to my side, trying to look small and nonthreatening. It was a hilarious fail, but I didn't tell him so.

I stopped in front of the Centaur, my face nearly level with the wound. "What gave you this?"

"A poisoned blade."

I nodded, inspecting the cut. "Did the poison smell of anything? Did it have a color?"

"It smelled of anise and was black."

Okay, so maybe a Morticella Poison. Hopefully. "I think I have something for it."

He waited in silence as I dug around in my potion belt. Like the antidote we'd just taken, I couldn't be sure it would work since I wasn't sure that it actually *was* infected with the Morticella Poison, but it shouldn't hurt him.

I handed it over. "You can spread it on your wound."

For one, I wasn't keen on touching it. And for another, he didn't look like the type who wanted to be touched.

The Centaur nodded and took the potion.

"What's your name?" I asked.

"Chiron."

"I'm Rowan, and this is Maximus."

He nodded. As he spread the potion on the wound, I figured that we should probably try to get some info out of this guy.

"Why are there so many booby traps in this forest?" I asked.

"To protect Medusa."

My brows jumped. "To protect *her*?"

Chiron looked at me like I was an idiot. "And to protect you."

"I don't see how dangling upside down from a snare protects me."

"You are approaching Medusa's lair. As you get closer, the traps become more dangerous. The point is to drive you off before you see her."

Suddenly, I understood. "Oh, so someone put them up to protect people from her."

"No." Disgust echoed in his voice. "I already told you, they are to protect her. You are protected as an afterthought. She doesn't want to be hunted, and she also doesn't want to turn anyone to stone."

"She doesn't?" Maximus asked.

"No." Sadness entered the Centaur's eyes. "I assume you were told the version of the myth where Medusa was born as a Gorgon and thrives on turning men to stone?"

Maximus nodded. So did I. There were several different versions of various myths, but that was the one I'd always heard about Medusa.

"Well, it's not true." Chiron shrugged. "It was the gods who turned her, through no fault of her own."

"What do you mean?" I asked.

"She was once a beautiful maiden. Blue eyes and golden hair. So fair that Poseidon himself became enamored of her. But she didn't want him. She didn't want anyone, for she had sworn herself to virtue in Athena's temple."

Athena was the virgin goddess, something I couldn't relate to myself, but hey, to each their own.

"What happened to her?" I asked as dread uncoiled in my stomach. One of my least favorite things about the Greek gods was how the male ones tended to fall into lust with women and then go after them, often without their consent.

"What usually happens." Disgust echoed in Chiron's voice. "Poseidon cornered her and raped her in Athena's temple. Athena was so enraged at Medusa that she turned her into the snake-haired Gorgon that she is today."

Horror welled within me. "What? Why didn't she go after Poseidon? Clearly he is the one in the wrong."

"The gods hold archaic beliefs." Chiron shook his head. "It's not the first instance of them being bastards, and it won't be the last."

He was right. The stories were full of the gods being awful— both the men and the women.

Poor Medusa.

What the hell was I supposed to do?

I looked at Maximus, torn. His brow was creased and his eyes shadowed.

"So now you see why I did not want you to hunt Medusa. She doesn't deserve it."

Damn, this sucked. "That's why she hides out in this forest. Of course."

I really wanted to turn into a dragon, damn it. But I wasn't going to kill some innocent woman to get there. True, she'd killed a lot of people. But she hadn't *wanted* to. And how awful to not be able to look upon someone without murdering them.

I scowled. "Shit."

"Why must you kill her?" Chiron asked. "Just turn back. Whatever the reason, it cannot be that compelling."

His words filled me with dread. This wasn't just about turning into a dragon because it was fun. It was about transforming into my final form—dragon or not—so I could take down the Titans and save the world. "But it can be that bad. It is."

Chiron gave me a skeptical look, and so I explained, telling him the whole story of the Titans and the chaos that could fill the world and destroy it.

Chiron's face paled and set in harsh lines. "The Titans."

"Do you hate them as well?" Maximus asked.

Chiron nodded sharply. "Pure evil, and determined to spread more of it." Sadness creased his features. "And the dragons say you must bring them Medusa's head to complete your transformation."

Tears pricked my eyes. I hadn't even met Medusa yet, but I knew I couldn't kill her. "I'm supposed to."

Was that the point of this challenge? They were going to make me do something truly terrible to prove I was strong enough to defeat the Titans? I had to kill an innocent to be worthy of those powers?

I hated that idea.

Despised it.

"Maybe the dragons don't know about Medusa's true nature," I said.

"They know," Chiron said.

"I can't do it. I won't." I shook my head fiercely, reaching into my pocket and gripping the white dragon claw that they'd given me. "There must be another way."

"You may not complete your final transformation," Chiron said. "The dragons do not go back on their word. They want what they want."

I scowled, my heart thundering. Medusa was innocent. I couldn't believe I had to kill her. I wouldn't.

Maximus's dire expression was softening into a smile.

"Why are you smiling?"

"They said *heads*." His gazed drilled into mine. "The dragons said that you must bring Medusa's heads."

"Plural?" Chiron asked.

"Yes." Maximus nodded. "I thought it was strange at the time, but perhaps it is a clue."

Hope flared in my chest.

Chiron grinned. "Ah, those dragons."

"What?" I asked.

"The challenge is so perfect. So dragon-like."

"What do you mean?"

"It tests your heart and your brain. Your empathy and your cleverness."

"Maybe they don't want me to kill Medusa?" Tension drained from my limbs as I clung to that idea. There was no way in Hades I'd kill her, and this could be my out.

I could still succeed.

"You just have to bring the heads," Maximus said.

"I don't think she'll let you cut her snakes' heads off," Chiron said.

"No, she probably won't." There was no way she wanted snakes for hair, but even if she didn't like the snakes themselves, it would hurt if I chopped all their heads off. I was going to have to figure something out.

"Your goal is important," Chiron said. "But the path beyond here is nearly impossible. No one has made it in millennia. Not since her guardian appeared."

"Guardian?" Maximus asked.

"The spider who devours souls." True fear echoed in his voice.

Ah, shit, that sounded bad. Especially the way he'd said it.

"The beast will surely end your life," Chiron said.

"I can't turn back."

Maximus nodded.

Chiron shrugged. "I've told you what I can. I'm confident you won't kill Medusa—probably because you will die before you reach her. But if not, best of luck to you. I hope you are not wrong."

"Me too."

"If you meet the Titans on the field of battle, call for me." He reached into a pouch at his side and withdrew a small silver stone. "Speak into this, and I will hear you. I'd like to join your battle, as would my brothers."

Hey, that was awesome. I took the silver rock and clutched it in my hand.

With that, he turned and cantered away, moving swiftly through the forest.

I looked at Maximus. "Well, shit."

"I agree that we cannot kill Medusa, even if the dragons wish it. My theory about the heads may be false, but I couldn't condone killing her, given what we know now."

"Good. Thank you." It helped to have him on my side. And I wasn't surprised he agreed with me. No way I could love someone who thought that killing Medusa was the right thing to do.

"Let's keep moving." Maximus raised his mirror. "We may need time to convince her we don't mean her harm."

"And time to fight whatever monster guards her." Chiron's lack of details made it even scarier.

We continued through the forest, moving as quickly as we could with our safety equipment slowing us down. We had to look ridiculous, but no way I was letting down my guard.

The faint whistle called us forward, and magic began to prickle against my skin as we cut deeper through the forest. Leaves appeared on the trees, casting more shade on the ground as they blocked the sun.

The farther we walked, the harder my heart pounded. What was this monster?

When the first bit of sticky white string struck me, I jumped. It twisted around my chest, binding my arms to my sides. Within seconds, a hundred more strands had wrapped themselves around me.

Panic iced my veins and made my head buzz with dull noise.

I thrashed, looking at Maximus, who was also bound tightly. We were trapped within a spider's webbing, which wound around both of us so tightly and thickly that we looked like flies waiting to be eaten.

I struggled, sweating and thrashing, but I couldn't break free. Maximus strained at the bonds, his face turning red and the veins popping out on his neck.

"I can't get out." His voice was rough.

He was strong enough to break through almost anything, but he couldn't get through this?

"Try harder." Panic made my voice high.

He fought the bindings, turning even redder, but nothing happened. "I can't break it."

He sounded almost bewildered. Maximus had never met something he couldn't muscle his way out of.

Shit, shit, shit.

I couldn't reach my potions—they were well trapped in my bag, squished against my body.

I almost screamed for Romeo and the Menacing Menagerie, but we couldn't bring them here. I'd only ever been able to send Romeo a wordless SOS for help, never been able to actually speak to him if he wasn't right next to me. If I couldn't explain the situation they were walking into, they'd get trapped just as quickly. I'd be inviting them to their deaths. No way I could do that.

I could explain the problem to my sisters over my comms charm, but I couldn't reach it to ignite the magic.

A hissing noise sounded from above, and my stomach dropped to my feet.

I looked up, spotting the many-eyed stare of an enormous black spider. The creature's long fangs dripped with venom. Hunger glinted in its eyes, and my skin chilled.

The spider that devours souls.

Oh, fates. Chiron had warned us.

The spider descended quickly, and my heart beat so strongly that I nearly passed out.

I looked at Maximus, who was as tightly bound as ever. If he couldn't get out of here, we were screwed.

The spider was only ten feet above us now. There was no cavalry, no way to break free, and no hope.

We're dead.

I did the only thing I could think of.

I looked at Maximus and blurted, "I love you."

His startled gaze jerked up to mine.

"I couldn't die without telling you that." In a normal circumstance, I might have blushed. Being about to die definitely removed any embarrassment, however.

Before he could speak, the spider hissed and landed in front of us.

9

T he spider's eyes darted between the two of us.

I cringed as I looked at it, so scared that I could barely breathe.

"Do you love her?" the spider hissed.

I blinked at it.

What the hell?

At that moment, an image of a woman's face flashed over the spider's head. I squinted at the creature. The apparition had disappeared, but the spider had definitely spoken.

Even now, interest gleamed in its eyes. I couldn't say which answer the spider expected or wanted, but it was curious.

It took everything I had to look from the spider to Maximus, but even in the face of death, I wanted to hear his words.

His gaze met mine. "Yes." He jerked a bit, clearly trying to shrug and failing because of the spider's tight bindings. "Once I met you, it was really only a matter of time."

Warmth glowed through me. Not enough to douse the terror that was about to make me wet myself, but it made it a bit easier to think.

Holy fates.

The spider had talked.

I should have cottoned on to the enormity of that sooner, but I wasn't at my best right now. But if it could talk, maybe we could convince it.

I turned back to it, the words coming out in a rush. "We're not here to hurt you or Medusa or anyone. We know her story. About how Poseidon raped her and Athena turned her into a monster. That's so wrong. We want to help her."

The spider looked at us, skepticism clear in its gaze. "Why?"

I explained about the Titans and my goal of completing my transition to full Dragon God. "So, you see, this is part of my journey."

The spider tapped its right front leg on the ground, clearly thinking. Again, the image of a woman's face flickered in front of the spider's head.

The dots suddenly connected for me. "Arachne?"

The spider nodded its head once. Arachne had once been a woman. The greatest weaver in ancient Greece, in fact. She'd been so bold about her skill that she had angered the Goddess Athena. The gods couldn't bear an assault on their pride, and a human being better than them at a skill was one of the worst insults.

I thought it was all rather stupid, really.

Especially since Athena had turned Arachne into a spider.

"It was wrong what happened to you too," I said. "I might be the Greek Dragon God, but I don't agree with how the gods have behaved always. They've done awful things, especially to women."

"It's terrible," Maximus said.

"We can try to help you," I said. "Find a way to turn you back to a human. That's our goal with Medusa."

Arachne seemed to sigh. She didn't make a noise, not the way a human would, but her spidery body seemed to relax.

"I do not want to change back." She raised her two front legs. "I did not like my lot at first, but I enjoy it now. No one can hurt me when I am in this form. I am the greatest weaver in all the land. And there's nothing Athena can do about it."

I grinned at her. "Good for you."

She inclined her head. "You're really not here to hurt Medusa?"

Maximus shook his head.

"No," I said. "When I thought she was a monster who enjoyed killing people, I thought I was supposed to kill her. When I learned her true story, however, I couldn't."

Arachne tapped her right leg against the ground, clearly her thinking gesture. I couldn't read expressions on her face other than getting a hint from her eyes, but she seemed to be weighing something heavily.

"I will miss Medusa in this forest," she said. "But she is not happy here. Not like I am. She hasn't been happy in forever. If you truly think you can help her, I will let you go."

"I think we can," I said.

Maximus tilted his head toward me. "Rowan can do anything with potions. I believe she can help Medusa."

Arachne nodded her head sharply. "Fine, then. I will release you and help you approach her. It will be difficult to get close, as she startles easily. You cannot let your gaze fall upon her. Or hers upon you."

"Wait, what?" I frowned. "I thought we were only turned to stone if we looked at her face."

"No. Over time, her magic has grown stronger. She can now kill with a look." The spider shook her head. "Honestly, I am no longer needed as her guardian."

Shit, shit, shit.

This had just become a lot more dangerous.

I looked at Maximus.

He only considered a moment before saying, "We still have to try."

I nodded. He was right, of course. Not only did the world rely upon us, but I really wanted to help Medusa. She didn't deserve this.

"I don't suggest that you approach by normal means," Arachne said. "She will be expecting it."

"Would she be waiting to turn us to stone?" Maximus asked.

"I don't think so," Arachne said. "At first, she hides. She doesn't want to turn anyone to stone. But if she must, she will."

"What if we approach from the sky?"

Arachne nodded. "I think that is smart. I will help you. Only I come from the sky, and I am good. Threats do not come from that direction, so it should buy you time to convince her you are a friend."

When I'd first seen Arachne, this was not how I'd expected things to go. I looked down at my arms, which were starting to turn numb from being bound so tightly to my sides. "Could you get us out of here?"

"Yes." Arachne approached, using her front legs to make quick work of untying the webbing.

I stepped away and shook my arms, grateful. She did Maximus next, and once he was free, he stepped back and met my gaze.

Memories of the words we'd said flashed in my mind. They were clearly running through his too.

"Let's go." Arachne started through the forest.

I gave Maximus one last look, then followed.

Arachne moved quickly, and we had to jog to keep up. She dodged around trees and took a circuitous route, turning back only once to say, "Follow closely to avoid the traps."

I saluted her and stuck close.

The trees began to fill out with even more leaves by the time we slowed. Medusa's forest was different from the rest—carefully cultivated and lovely.

It made sense, though. If she was out here all alone, with just Arachne for company, of course she'd need a hobby.

"I think we should start to ascend here," Arachne said. "The branches are strong enough."

I looked up, spotting a thick canopy of large branches.

"Once we've reached her home, I will help you descend with my web," Arachne said. "But you may want to carry some kind of shield to keep her gaze from falling on you directly."

"I can conjure something once we are up," Maximus said.

"If she presents you with the back of her head, then it is safe to look upon her. It is only her human eyes that will turn you to stone. The snakes do not have that power."

Okay, that would make this a tiny bit easier.

Arachne began to climb, and we followed. My heart thundered as we ascended. This was going to be tough.

The tree bark was rough under my hands, thick and knobby. It made it easy to climb, and soon, we were high amongst the branches.

"This way." Arachne moved as gracefully as a swan in the water, creeping over the tops of the tree branches to reach Medusa's home.

We were slower and clumsier, but we managed to follow. Soon, a flash of white marble appeared below.

A path. Then a small building. A fountain.

"We're nearly there," Arachne said.

Finally, we reached a clearing. I caught the briefest glance of a little settlement before yanking my gaze up. I didn't want them to fall unexpectedly upon Medusa. I tried to memorize what I'd seen, though, since I'd need that info later. There had been three small marble buildings surrounding it, remnants of ancient

Greece hidden deep in the forest. A fountain had splashed in the middle.

"Get your shields," Arachne said.

"Does it matter how thick the shield is?" Maximus asked. "It's only meant to protect us from her sight, correct?"

"Correct."

Maximus grinned and conjured two enormous umbrellas. "These will cover the most."

He handed me a colorful umbrella. Arachne began to eject webbing from her hind end. It was a bit strange to watch, but beggars couldn't be choosers.

She handed me an end of the fine silver webbing, and I took it, wincing slightly at the stickiness.

"Tie it around your waist."

I did as she commanded, not daring to look at the ground below. Maximus did the same, and soon we had our umbrellas open.

I glanced at Maximus. "I feel like I'm in the circus."

He grinned.

"Medusa!" Arachne called. "You have visitors!"

There was silence. My heart began to thunder.

"Medusa!"

More silence.

"She can hear us," Arachne said. "She never goes far from here, so she must be able to."

"Maybe she is frightened?" I asked.

"Likely," Arachne said.

"We know your story, Medusa," I shouted. "It's dreadfully unfair. We're here to help you."

"You know nothing," a voice shouted. Anger and fear echoed in it.

Dang, those were two dangerous combinations.

"We know about Poseidon and Athena. What they did was wrong."

"The gods no longer rule," Maximus said. "You do not have to worry about them."

Medusa laughed bitterly.

This was going nowhere. I looked at Arachne. "Can you lower us to the forest floor?"

"If you think that's wise."

"I do." I turned back to the forest floor to project my voice that way, though I could no longer see past the umbrellas. "We're going to join you, Medusa! But we will not attack. Please, just come speak to us."

"If I look upon you, you will die."

"I saw no statues when I looked at your home a moment ago," I said. "You don't seem to be killing many people."

"I dispose of the statues. I do not like them."

I couldn't blame her. I wouldn't want artwork reminders of all the demons I'd killed in the line of duty.

"Well, either way, we're approaching. If we meant you harm, we would not announce our presence. And your friend Arachne would not trust us."

"I do trust them," Arachne said.

"All right." Medusa didn't sound pleased about it, but she didn't sound super pissed, at least. There might have even been a bit of hope in her voice.

"Let's go," Maximus said.

We leaned off the branch, dangling in thin air with our umbrellas pointed downward. Arachne deployed her web, lowering us slowly to the forest floor.

"Nearly there!" Arachne said.

When my umbrella hit the ground below, I lifted it, careful to keep it in front of me.

"We're here, Medusa! Come out and speak to us."

"All right. But I will approach you backward."

I waited, shifting uncomfortably as I used my animal hearing to get a sense of what she was doing. Soft footsteps sounded on the forest floor.

"She is standing in the clearing," Arachne said. "And she is not facing you. It is safe to lower your umbrellas and look upon her."

I sucked in a deep breath and glanced at Maximus. He nodded, and we lowered our umbrellas. My heart threatened to beat its way out of my chest, and I had my eyes squeezed so tightly closed that it almost hurt.

Though, in all honesty, it didn't matter that much if I looked upon her. She could give me one look, and I'd be stone.

Slowly, I opened my eyes.

A woman stood with her back toward us. Green snakes writhed on her head, hissing and glaring.

Oh fates, that was awful.

I would hate to live like that.

We had to help her. But how?

Maybe she would have an idea.

"Tell me exactly how you found me," Medusa said. "What leads you to my lair?"

"Well, I'm on a quest."

She laughed bitterly. "They all are."

"True. But this one doesn't involve killing you. I thought it did, but once I heard your story, I knew I couldn't do it."

She shrugged. "Tell me more."

I explained about the dragons and the claw dagger they'd given me.

"Throw it to me," Medusa said. "I want to see it."

Was there excitement in her voice? I dug into my pocket and removed the sparkling opalescent claw. I tossed it to her in a perfect arc, quite proud of myself when it sailed down in front of her, and she snagged it out of the air.

"It is the dagger of choice." Now it was clear that excitement echoed in her voice. "It could kill me or save me, depending upon your intentions."

"Oh fates. So if I'd chosen wrong, I really could have killed you."

"But you didn't choose wrong," Maximus said.

"How can it save you, though?" I asked.

The snakes continued to hiss at me, glaring even more fiercely. If they understood English, they didn't like the direction this conversation was taking.

"It magnifies your intentions. It could turn back the curse if you so wished." Her voice turned doubtful at the end of her sentence. "Though I'm not sure that wishes are enough."

I chewed on my lower lip as I thought. "What if I have a potion that breaks spells?"

I'd only ever used it to break the protection spells on locked doors, but it could work for this.

"That might do it." Excitement echoed in her voice. "What if you put it on the dagger and pierce me with it?"

"That seems a bit extreme," Maximus said.

"Living with snakes on your head for thousands of years is a bit extreme. If this gets me out of that, you're welcome to stab me in the heart."

"Maybe not the heart." I reached for my potion belt and pulled out the tiny vial of spell breaker. There was no way it alone could break a god's spell, but maybe with this fancy dragon claw dagger. "I've got the potion."

"I'll throw back the dagger." She lobbed it into the air, aiming closer to Maximus.

He darted left to grab it, snagging it easily.

"Are you sure about this?" Arachne asked.

"I am." There was a smile in Medusa's voice. "It's worth the risk, even if I die. Any hope at all is worth the risk. And think of it, old friend. I'll finally be able to look at you again!"

"That would be nice. Promise you'll come visit."

"I will."

Oh fates, I hoped this worked. Medusa had been trapped for so long. If I killed her by accident...

I couldn't live with myself, frankly.

"Okay, I'm going to approach you from behind," I said.

"Do whatever you have to." Her voice turned thoughtful. "Perhaps you should stab me in the left arm. I don't use that one much."

"All right." I approached her slowly, Maximus at my side. As we neared the snakes, they began to hiss and writhe more violently.

"By the way, Medusa. I think I'm supposed to bring the heads of your snakes to the dragons to prove what I have done."

"If you turn me back to normal, you can have the little bastards. They're not even really alive. They don't eat or sleep or anything. Pure dark magic is what they are."

"It's a deal." I held out my hand for the dagger, and Maximus passed it to me.

The dragon claw was cool in my palm, sparking with magic. I uncorked the vial of spell breaker and dripped it over the point of the dragon claw. The liquid gleamed blue in the light.

"Okay, I'm going to stab you." I didn't usually give a warning.

Medusa didn't even flinch, though. I had a feeling that she'd accept being skinned alive to get out of this curse.

I raised the dagger over her arm, framing my intentions in my mind. If this dagger was going to magnify them, I didn't want it getting confused.

Turn her back to human.

I thrust the claw downward, piercing the fleshy outer bit that

I doubted had any important ligaments or whatever made arms move.

Medusa winced and hissed in pain. Magic burst from the blade, flowing outward over Medusa in waves of golden light.

The snakes on her head went wild, hissing and thrashing. When the light reached them, they froze. One by one, they fell off of her head, disconnecting from her scalp. In their place appeared golden hair, long and straight.

Holy fates, it was working!

Excitement burst in my chest. I could hear Arachne up above, giving a weird little spider shriek of delight.

"It's working!" Medusa said.

All of the snakes were off her head now. She reached up to touch her face, then gave a little jump.

"My face is back to normal! My nose! My cheeks!"

"Does this mean you won't turn us to stone?" Maximus asked.

"I think not." She spun around before I could dodge left or right.

Horrified, I stared into her eyes.

They were a beautiful blue. And her face was beautiful, too.

Even better, I was still breathing. I moved my arms.

Yep, not a statue.

Oh, thank fates.

It was stupid that her beauty made her good and her ugliness had made her bad—they weren't things that should be equated. But the Greek gods weren't exactly advanced thinkers. Her beauty had drawn Poseidon to her, and ugliness with a side helping of the stone curse had been Athena's best punishment.

"You saved me!" Medusa threw her arms around me.

I grinned and hugged her back.

At my side, Maximus conjured a small bag, then bent and collected the dead snakes that lay withered on the ground.

I pulled back from Medusa. "Do you know where you will go now?"

She moved away from me and looked up at the trees, her gaze landing on Arachne. A beautiful smile brightened her face. "I'll spend time with my old friend. From there, we shall see."

Arachne waved at her with one of her front legs, and my heart warmed.

Man, sometimes I really liked my job.

"If you ever need help, you can come to the Undercover Protectorate in Scotland. Just go to the Whiskey and Warlock pub in Edinburgh. They'll direct you there."

Medusa squeezed my arm. "Thank you. Truly."

I nodded. "I'm just glad I met the Centaur Chiron so he could tell me your true story."

Otherwise, I'd have killed her. The idea made my stomach turn. It was so dangerous to run around on quests where the goal was to kill people. How were you to know you were even doing the right thing?

I shivered. Lesson learned for the future.

I looked at Maximus. "Ready to go back?"

"Yes. But how? They transported us here."

As soon as he said the word, the ether began to pull at me. The dragons were calling us back.

I gave Arachne and Medusa one last look, then the ether sucked me in.

Fates, I hope we did this right.

We arrived back in the ceremonial center of Olympus. The wind whipped coldly over my cheeks, and I gripped the dragon's claw tightly in my hands.

Next to me, Maximus carried the bag of snake heads.

I spun in a quick circle, taking in the dragons. All six stared at us, interest gleaming in their jewel-like eyes. I really hated how they'd laid out this space. It'd be so much better to face the dragons head-on. Instead, I had to choose which one to face.

Obviously, it had to be Ladon.

"Well?" Ladon asked.

I nodded to Maximus, who dumped the snake heads onto the ground.

"At first, I thought I was supposed to kill Medusa," I said. "Everything I'd ever heard about her was bad."

"I know," Ladon said.

I didn't ask *how* he'd known. He was a damned dragon. They knew stuff.

"Along the way, we learned her story," I continued. "I knew I couldn't kill her, then. Even if I'd had to kill her, I wouldn't have. But Maximus remembered what you said about *heads*. Plural." I nodded down to the withered snakes on the ground. They still stank of dark magic, and some of them had turned entirely to dust. "I hope we were right about that."

"You were indeed," Ladon said. "We had hoped you would choose the right path. A Drakaina is powerful—we wouldn't give that power to someone who couldn't wield it well."

"Drakaina?" I asked.

He nodded. "A female dragon."

My heart began to pound and my head to spin. Was he saying what I thought he was saying?

Please let him be saying that. Oh, please!

The six dragons raised their wings, magic sparking around them. Red, yellow, white, blue, green. Every color glittered in the air, and the dragons roared. It shook my eardrums, nearly sending me to my knees.

I stiffened my legs, determined not to fall in front of them. I would be worthy.

The magic surged toward me, slamming into me like a freight train. Because it came from all directions, I didn't fall over. Instead, it lifted me up, filling me with so much power that I thought my head might pop off. I could barely breathe, and every muscle began to tear.

Pain streaked through me, along with a weird kind of pleasure. Almost like triumph.

My vision began to darken, the sparkling magic glittering at the edges. A moment later, power exploded from me, making me feel like a supernova.

I shot into the air, feeling *amazing.*

I was strength.

I was grace.

I was power.

I was *dragon.*

Massive wings flapped alongside me, brilliant silver in the

sun. The magic that flowed through me felt like a homecoming, and I soared upward, the wind against my face.

Joy burst in my chest.

But only for a second.

My wings faltered. Suddenly, the air felt like pudding. It was impossible to fly through it. I collapsed backward and slammed onto the ground.

Pain surged in my skull, and I blinked, swearing that I saw stars circling my head as if I were in an old cartoon.

I struggled upright, flopping around on my dragon feet, my wings as awkward as two umbrellas in the wind.

Oh fates.

I was a terrible dragon.

I turned my head to look at both my wings. They were huge and magnificent, silvery and sparkling in the sun. They looked like they should carry me to the moon.

In reality, they'd carried me about twenty feet up, and most of that had probably been because of the magic of the other dragons.

Boy, I was going to need some practice.

I was like an awkward adolescent dragon who'd just gone through a growth spurt and stumbled around like a giant.

It was a letdown to not be soaring through the skies like a professional, but only for half a second.

Because holy fates, I was a dragon!

A dragon who needed some practice. But I was a freaking dragon!

Wait until my sisters see this.

I should blow some fire. That was very dragon-y and a skill I really ought to have.

For safety's sake, I raised my head to look toward the sky. I didn't want to barbecue anyone, after all. I called upon the heat that I felt within my chest. It was like there was a furnace inside me, constantly pumping fire through my veins.

I forced the heat to rise from my chest through my throat, and I blew it outward.

A puff of smoke escaped from my lips. *Maybe* a tiny little flame.

Dang.

My shoulders sagged, but only a millimeter.

I looked down at Maximus, who was looking at me with an expression of such awe that my shoulders went up again.

I would get the hang of this.

I'd have to.

I turned to look at Ladon, who looked a little impressed himself.

"You look good," he said.

I tried to speak, but no words came out.

"You'll have to shift back," he said. "You are not quite like us. At least, not yet. With practice, you may be able to speak in your dragon form. But not now."

I nodded, then imagined turning back into my human self. It took a few moments, but the magic surged through my limbs finally, shrinking me back down to human size.

I looked down at myself, spotting my usual shirt, jacket, and jeans. Thank fates I still wore my clothes. Transforming back naked would be a real pain. I shot a glance up at Zeus's castle to see if he was watching. He was, and his expression was conflicted.

I looked up at Ladon. "Is it normal for me to be so...awkward?"

Ladon shrugged an enormous shoulder. "I have no idea. A human has never transformed into a dragon before."

Wow.

"It is true, though. You need practice." Ladon grimaced. "A lot of practice."

"No kidding." The memory of flopping back down to the ground in front of all these dragons made my cheeks warm. "I don't have a lot of time, though."

"You aren't getting any more, so work hard."

Maximus approached me, stopping to stand by my side. He looked at the dragons. "We do have one other problem."

"And what is that?" Ladon asked.

"We don't yet have a way to put the Titans back in Tartarus."

"I'm not sure we can help with that," he said. "But I do have a warning for you, Rowan."

Uh-oh. "Yes?"

"The darkness in you is still there."

A shiver of dread raced over me. "I know. But I've come to terms with it."

"Good. Because you will be tested once more. One final time. The pull of evil and power is strong. Too much for most people to resist. It could make you the most powerful being in existence, but you must not embrace it."

My mind snagged on the "most powerful being" part. Was that how I was supposed to defeat the Titans? I had to become mega powerful to do it?

Except, I couldn't embrace the darkness.

Ladon had made that clear, and I was unwilling to anyway. I didn't want to be like them. How could I come back from that? Could I, even?

"You must be careful, Rowan." Ladon's eyes burned into me. "Everything relies on you, but you must choose the right way. Or you will lose everything you love."

～

The dragons sent Maximus and me back to the Protectorate castle using their magic. When we arrived, the moon hung high overhead, gleaming brilliantly on the castle walls.

"I lost track of time," I said.

Maximus rubbed a hand over his face, weariness in the gesture. "It's been a while since we've slept."

Adrenaline had kept me going before this, but it was wearing off now. Fast. From the look of the moon, it was the middle of the night. Which meant we'd been awake for twenty-four hours, all of which had been spent running and fighting and using magic.

I was so tapped out that a bowl of pudding would be stronger than me.

The castle was quiet now, incredibly so. Everyone had to be asleep. Or at least, everyone except the guards.

"Let's go check the wall and see if the army is still out there," I asked.

"We can ask the guards where everyone is, too."

I reached for Maximus's hand, and we started across the castle lawn, striding toward the exterior curtain wall.

I took the stairs two at a time, hurrying to the top of the ramparts. Fatigue filled every inch of my body as I moved. It was almost as if coming home and being safe made me realize how damned tired I was.

When I reached the top, I looked out over the forest that surrounded the castle. Hundreds of demons and humans still stood there, staring at us.

For the briefest second, adrenaline flooded my veins. Then it sapped away, and I was left shakier than ever.

But damn, the Titans were determined.

Caro and Ali approached from the left, gray circles under their eyes. They were clearly almost as exhausted as we were, but no way they'd fall asleep on guard duty.

Ali ran a hand through his shiny dark hair. He looked a lot like Aladdin from that kids' movie. Slender and handsome and young. He was a Djinn with the power to possess the bodies of people and animals, and he was a badass fighter with that skill.

I'd hardly seen him lately, though. Hell, I'd hardly seen most of my friends. I couldn't wait for the day where we could just hang out again.

But for now, we had a war to win.

"They haven't moved at all?" I asked.

"Not a bit." Caro shook her head, her short platinum bob shining in the light. "They just stare at us like a bunch of crazies."

"They'd have to be crazy to follow the Titans," Maximus said.

"Truth." Ali grinned. "Did you have any luck?"

"Yes. But I'll show you tomorrow." If I tried to turn into a dragon right now, I'd definitely fall off the ramparts. "Where is everyone?"

"Asleep," Caro said. "It's one a.m., and most people haven't slept in days. Several teams made progress over the last twenty-four hours, though, so everyone is resting up."

"Perfect." We'd gotten here just in time. Because damn, I really needed to join the team slumber party.

"Is there a meeting scheduled for tomorrow, then?" Maximus asked.

"Yep. Seven a.m. sharp. Kitchens." Ali grinned again, this time even wider. "Can't say I mind having our meetings where the food is."

Caro laughed, though the sound was weighty with weariness, and punched him lightly on the shoulder. "Of course you don't. You'd eat an old leather shoe and say it tasted good."

"With the right seasoning, it could."

Hmm, the way he was looking at her made this really seem

like flirting. *Interesting.* "Okay, we're going to head to bed, then. Unless you need us to cover for you up here?"

The idea made me want to cry, but I couldn't leave my friends hanging if they were as exhausted as I was.

"Nope. We already got a good nap in," Ali said. "We're fine."

"Awesome. See you later, and good luck."

Maximus and I climbed down the stairs and started across the lawn toward the castle. Several of the mullioned windows gleamed like crystal, but most were dark.

It didn't take us long to reach my apartment. The Menacing Menagerie were asleep on the couch, the three of them snoring in tandem. We tiptoed past them and fell into bed, barely managing to get off our shoes and outerwear.

I rolled over toward Maximus and laid my head on his chest. Memories of our time with Arachne flashed in my mind.

"Did you mean it?" I blurted. "When you said you loved me, did you mean it?"

He looked down, surprise on his handsome face. "Of course I meant it."

He sounded so sure, and almost a little offended that I would even ask, that I smiled.

I snuggled closer to him. "Good. I meant it, too."

"I know you meant it." There was a smile in his voice. "You blurted it out like they were the last words you'd ever say."

"I thought they would be." The thought of that feeling shivered through me. It may have all turned out well, but that brief moment had been *awful.*

I wanted to talk more, but exhaustion pulled at me. It must have tugged at him, too, because he was silent.

As I drifted off to sleep, I thought of what Ladon had said about the darkness inside of me. What exactly had he meant by all that?

Was the darkness inside me really under control like I

thought it was? Or had my acceptance of it just been a clever trick by my subconscious?

The next morning, Maximus and I visited the ramparts again before the meeting with the rest of the Protectorate. The army was still there, staring silently at us.

"What do you want to bet this group can appear at the Titans' fortress within minutes if they call them?" I asked.

"Not taking that bet." Maximus rubbed a hand against his chin. "But since you're right, it'd probably be smart to find a way to trap them here so we don't have to fight them along with the Titans."

"Yeah. The Titans already had a pretty big human and demon army when I saw them last. I bet it's only grown."

"We'll figure something out." Maximus took my hand, and we walked back down the stairs, off the ramparts.

I'd finished my transition, but there was so much left to face. Not just an enormous army, but also my iffy skill with my new form.

"We have a few minutes before the meeting," I said. "I think I'm going to practice transforming."

"Good idea." Maximus squeezed my hand.

"Don't sound so relieved." I grinned. "But I guess if you have a dragon on your side, it's good if that dragon can do more than flop around."

"I'd still love you if all you could do was flop."

I laughed and let go of his hand. "I'm going to be the best dragon you ever saw."

"I don't doubt it."

Fates, I hoped I could live up to my big words.

I stopped in the middle of the castle lawn and drew in a deep breath. There was no one outside right now except the guards on the castle wall. I'd checked, and it was no longer Ali and Caro, but rather some members of the Demon Hunters Unit that I didn't know well.

Actually....

I looked at Maximus. "Will you go tell the guards not to shoot me if they see me in dragon form?"

"On it." He loped back toward the wall to deliver the message.

Once I was alone, I drew in another breath. The quiet helped. Being alone with no one watching helped even more, actually.

It was just me and the dragon inside me, and we weren't going to flop around like a fish out of water.

I called upon the dragon magic in my soul, feeling it spark along my veins. It was so strong and obvious, a different kind of magic than I'd ever felt before. Sometimes it was hard to call new magic to the surface, but not this. It was almost as if this magic had been waiting within me forever, ready to burst free.

It surged through my veins, rising to the surface in a rush. Magic glittered around me, a rainbow of color that flowed in front of my face, whirling like a tornado.

Within a second, I could feel my body expand. Wings grew, claws formed, my muscles became huge. Soon, my head was level with the second story of the castle. Two shocked faces peered out at me.

Uh-oh.

Now I had an audience.

I shoved the worry away and focused on how amazing it was to finally *be* a dragon. A dragon!

I used that awe and joy to propel myself upward into the sky. This time, I flew a little higher. Fifty feet, at least.

Then, my wings faltered.

I fell, plummeting back to earth and hitting the ground hard. *Damn it.*

I climbed to my feet and tried again, surging upward on my wings. They were more than big enough. I wasn't some big-assed dragon with tiny wings. I mean, I had some pretty big hindquarters, but I also had huge wings. I just needed to learn to use them.

I clawed my way upward, pumping my wings hard. My breath heaved in my lungs and little puffs of smoke burst from my lips, but I didn't make it much farther this time either. Maybe sixty feet, at most. Considering I was at least thirty feet long, that was more like a jump than flying.

I hit the ground again, this time with a harder thud.

When I looked up, the entirety of the Protectorate was standing on the front steps of the castle. Every single one was staring at me. I swallowed hard.

Perfect. Just perfect.

11

The entire staff of the Protectorate stared at me. Most of them were holding juice boxes and bacon sandwiches, so they'd clearly come from the meeting in the kitchen.

Which I was now probably late for. I must have lost track of time while trying to fly.

I shifted back to my human form, insanely grateful to still be wearing clothes. The only thing worse than falling on your ass in front of your colleagues was then appearing naked afterward.

"Wow." Jude nodded. "That's cool."

I grinned at her. "Yeah. I just need to learn to fly and shoot fire and stuff."

"If you even *can*," Lavender said snidely.

I glowered at my old nemesis. I hadn't been in class lately, but the reason was obvious. Fighting the Titans was pretty much a full-time job. Lavender didn't like it though.

And I didn't like that her words echoed a very real fear of mine. What if I *couldn't* do it?

I shook the thought away. I couldn't let her see weakness, couldn't let her see that I cared. So I just shrugged. "Even if I can't, I'm still thirty feet long with giant fangs and claws, so I won't be totally useless in a battle."

Bree and Ana huffed out identical laughs.

"Okay, that's enough," Jude said. "We need to discuss the next steps. We've all got our breakfast, so let's go to the Round Room."

The crowd turned and filed in through the castle doors. Bree and Ana caught up with me, Cade and Lachlan at their sides.

"You're a dragon!" Bree whispered.

"That's so cool!" Ana said. "A freaking dragon!"

"Only if I can learn to fly and shoot fire and actually *be* a dragon." Most of my little speech to Lavender had been bravado.

"Oh, you'll get the hang of it." Ana waved her hand to indicate it was nothing.

"Yeah, you'll learn in no time," Bree said.

"I sure hope you're right." I looked at Bree. "Did you get the power source in Thailand? The one that the Titans were after to power their bind-breaking device?"

Bree's expression turned grim. "No. They beat me to it. By an hour, no more."

"Oh damn." That burned. And made my skin chill with nerves.

The Titans were one step closer to their goal. We'd known going after the power source was a longshot, but still, I'd hoped we'd succeed. The clock was really ticking down now.

"Don't worry." Ana patted Bree's arm. "We'll figure it out."

"Yeah, we will." The scent of bacon caught my nose, and my gaze zeroed in on the steps that led down to the kitchen. My stomach grumbled. "I'll catch up with you in the Round Room."

I glanced at Maximus, and he nodded as if he'd read my mind. Together, we raced down the kitchen stairs. Hans turned from his position at the stove and grinned, his mustache twitching.

"You're in a hurry!" He'd always been good about noticing those things.

I'd barely stepped into the kitchen itself when he grabbed two juice boxes and chucked them at us. We each snagged one out of the air. He then grabbed two paper-wrapped sandwiches and threw them in a perfect arc.

I grabbed mine, delighted to feel that it was still warm, and smiled at him. "Thanks, Hans. You're the best."

"Thank you," Maximus said.

Hans grinned and waved his hands. "Go, go! Save the world."

"We'll try." I turned and raced up the stairs, Maximus behind me.

We sprinted toward the round room, and I did my best to ignore the scent of bacon that wafted from the sandwich.

We slipped into the Round Room just as the last person was taking their seat. We found two free spots at the table and sat. Quickly, I unwrapped my sandwich and took a bite, nearly groaning at the salty-savory taste of the bacon. The sandwich was huge, and I said a quick prayer of thanks to Hans.

"All right," Jude said. "Clearly, Rowan has made some progress in her transition."

"Just a bit of practice to go," I said, trying to sound confident. Memories of flopping to my butt flashed through my head.

"Then let's get the bad news out of the way first." Jude clapped her hands together. "We failed to retrieve the power source that will power the Titans' bind-breaking device. It was impossible—they were ahead of us all along, so there was nothing we could do."

I liked that she didn't blame Bree. And how could she? Bree was one of the most powerful supernaturals in existence. If she couldn't do it, then it couldn't be done. Simple as that.

"So," Jude said. "That means they are moving ahead with their plan. But don't worry. We're moving ahead with ours."

Okay, it was hard not to worry, but I liked Jude's no-nonsense, forge-ahead attitude.

"We've located the Titans' fortress using your directions, Rowan," Jude said. "We've had recon teams out there looking for a way to get our army in. They haven't had any luck, but we're getting closer."

Cade, Bree's boyfriend, leaned forward. He was a jack-of-all-trades at the Protectorate and always took the most dangerous jobs. "As for the army, we're working on that. Our numbers are growing, but we need more."

"I think I have a few to add to the mix." I told them about the Centaurs and the Cyclopes.

Cade nodded, a pleased expression on his face. "That will be immensely helpful. When it comes time for battle, we'll get a message to them."

"They'll enjoy that."

"That leaves our biggest problem—figuring out how to get the Titans back into Tartarus."

"I believe we can help with that." The familiar voice sounded from behind me, near the door.

I turned, spotting Queens Penthesilea and Hippolyta. This was only their second visit to the Protectorate.

"Impressive timing," Jude said.

"We planned it that way." Queen Penthesilea grinned.

"No we didn't." Queen Hippolyta nudged her sister with her shoulder. "We just got lucky."

Queen Penthesilea chuckled. "Fine, that is the truth of it."

They strode into the room. Before I could stand to give my seats to them, a couple of guys from the Demon Hunters Unit had vacated theirs. They looked at the queens with starry eyes. I couldn't blame them. The Amazons were all strong and smart and hot. Pretty irresistible, really.

The queens sat gracefully, then turned to look from Jude to me.

"We've discovered that there is a way to put the Titans back into Tartarus, but it won't be easy," Queen Penthesilea said.

I leaned forward. "How?"

Queen Hippolyta met my gaze. "You must visit Hera and hear it from her directly. We've gained her permission to give you her location. And if you are worthy, you will leave with the way to trap the Titans."

Always with the worthiness. It was enough to give a girl a complex. But I just nodded. "Okay, I'll do it."

"I suggest you bring backup," Queen Hippolyta said. "Quite a bit of it."

Immediately, I looked at both my sisters. Sometime in the past couple weeks, it'd become a given that Maximus would come with me. But they also always had my back whenever I asked.

Both of them nodded immediately.

"A couple more wouldn't hurt," Queen Penthesilea said.

"I volunteer," Cade said at the same time Lachlan raised his hand.

"That settles it," Jude said. "The six of you will go to Hera. The rest of us will continue to build the army and plan our ambush. When you've returned, we'll attack."

My lips tugged up in a grim smile, and I nodded. "Let's get this over with."

Queen Hippolyta gave us the directions to reach Hera—who apparently no longer lived with Zeus on his mountain—and Lachlan created a portal for us to use.

I stepped into the ether, gasping as the magic sucked me in

and spun me around. It spat me out on a tropical beach. Warm wind blew through my hair, and the scent of the sea caressed my skin. I raised my face to the sun and sighed, closing my eyes.

"I think I need a margarita," I murmured.

"I need a week here," Bree said.

I opened my eyes and looked around. The place was gorgeous—white sands, blue water lapping at the shore, the sound of tropical birds. The sun sparkled on the surface, creating thousands of diamonds that nearly blinded me.

I didn't care though. I could stare at it for hours. Preferably from a hammock. With that margarita and a good book. Hell, I wouldn't even care if it was a bad book at this point.

I needed a vacation.

We all did.

Everyone I knew looked like they'd just finished the tax season while working at an accounting firm.

"Hera sure knows how to live," Maximus said.

"This is better than Olympus." I checked out the palm trees that drooped over the water, looking like a postcard. "And she never had a great relationship with Zeus anyway."

"Whoa," Ana said. "Look at that."

I turned around to follow her voice and spotted the gleaming white house peeking out from the trees. I hadn't noticed it before—I'd been too caught up in dreams of cocktails and beach naps—but now that I spotted it, my jaw dropped.

It was *beautiful.*

"Talk about a dream home." My gaze traveled over the huge windows that were open to the breeze and the massive white porch fitted with turquoise couches that were positioned to perfectly take in the view of the ocean. "Let's go meet the lady of the manor."

"And maybe make best friends with her," Bree said. "You know, so we can come back for weekends and girls' nights."

I nodded, liking that idea.

As we approached the house, the six of us began to walk more heavily. Normally, we were light-footed. But the last thing we wanted to do was sneak up on a god.

"Hello?" I called. "Hera? It's Rowan Blackwood. Queen Hippolyta and Queen Penthesilea sent me here."

"Hang on!" A frazzled voice came from inside the house, and it sounded nothing like what I would expect from one of the most powerful goddesses in the Greek pantheon.

A moment later, a woman ran out of the front door. Her blonde hair was tied in a messy knot on her head, and her face was streaked with blue paint. Unlike all the other gods I'd seen, she wore modern clothes. Blue yoga pants complemented a flowered tank top, and she grinned when she spotted us.

"Rowan. Glad you made it." She gestured for us to come forward. "Would you like some lemonade?"

"Sure." I glanced at my friends, and they were equally surprised.

We approached. Up close, Hera appeared to be in her late forties or early fifties, and she looked spectacular. She had a glow that I rarely saw on people in the city.

It appeared that divorce was treating her well.

She turned and led us into her kitchen. It was a gorgeous, modern space. Not super-space modern, with tons of chrome and metal. More like beachy modern, where everything was new and worked well and gleamed with a bright white sheen.

I'd crap this place up with potions in a heartbeat, but I liked looking at it.

"Take a seat." She gestured to the large island counter, and we each sat on one of the barstools while she poured some lemonade.

I wanted to tell her that we needed to get a move on—the Titans waited for no woman—but I didn't want to piss her off before she helped us. We could afford a few minutes, and I prayed this wouldn't go over that.

She finished filling the glasses and brought the tray to the island. "Made it myself."

"Thanks." I took a glass and sipped, wincing at the sour bite. I tried to give her my best smile, and I could feel my friends doing the same. Cade coughed low in his throat, nearly choking.

Hera took a sip, then spat it out. "Crap, that's shit, isn't it?"

"Um…" I nodded. "Yeah."

She set down her glass. "Well, you win some, you lose some." She leaned forward. "I've been taking up hobbies, you see. Now that I'm a free woman and all. So far I've knitted three ugly scarves, baked some flat soufflés, and made shitty lemonade. The painting isn't half bad, though." She touched her cheek where the paint sliced across it.

"Doesn't sound like a bad life though," Maximus said.

She grinned. "Indeed, it is not. I cut that lying philanderer loose, and I've never been happier."

I liked Hera. She'd surely done some terrible things in her past—all the gods had—but she seemed all right now. As long as I didn't look too closely under the surface.

"Queen Penthesilea and Queen Hippolyta said that you could tell me how to get the Titans into Tartarus," I said. "We're planning to attack their fortress, but we don't know what to do once we've got them. They're too powerful for a prison on earth."

Hera nodded. "Only Tartarus can hold them. But it won't be easy."

"What do we need to do?"

"You must go to the Cave of Treasures to retrieve a vessel that is capable of holding the Titans' souls. It is small and gold—you'll know it when you see it. Once you have that and you've put their souls into the vessel, I will take it to Tartarus. You can do whatever you want with their bodies." She grinned evilly. "I suggest upholstering some couches."

"Um, that's not a bad idea." I nodded slowly, trying to process how she'd gotten from disposing of dead Titans to upholstered couches. She was probably more of a sociopath than I'd realized.

"How do we get their souls into the vessel?" Maximus asked.

Hera pointed at me. "That is up to her."

Ah, shit. "I don't know how."

"Figure it out. It's your fated task, after all."

Double shit. "No hints?"

"Where is the fun in that?" She raised her brows, an incredulous look on her face.

"Well, it would be fun to rid the earth of a threat that will destroy it. I think that's really fun." I realized that my words were kind of snarky, so I smiled, trying to look nice. Or dumb. Whatever expression would make her not be pissed at me.

Didn't work.

She scowled. "It's your job, Rowan. Do it."

"I can do it." But her words made me wonder... "Why are the gods not more interested in defeating the Titans themselves? You were once great enemies."

"And surely you have a stake in it if the world goes to hell?" Bree asked.

"In fact, we don't have much stake." Hera swept out her arms, gesturing to her house. "I live in Annatlia, the godly realm. All of the gods live here, except for Zeus, who is crouched up on his mountain like some monster." Her eyes darkened at the sound of his name. "If the world goes to hell, it won't affect us."

"What about all the people who will die?" Maximus asked.

She shrugged. "They no longer worship us."

So, screw 'em, yeah?

That was clearly her thought process. The gods were all

about worship. Even the Titans wanted it. I looked around the room, catching the eyes of my sisters and Cade and Lachlan. They looked as unimpressed as I felt, but were clearly trying to hide it.

"Anyway," Hera said. "The gods are all busy with their own hobbies. It's been millennia since we've worked together. We'd probably get our asses kicked."

"Seriously?" I asked.

She nodded. "Not that seriously. We've got some powerful magic, after all, but those Titans are *intense*. It's just not worth the risk to us. They can't bother us in our realm and we no longer leave it, so it's really the perfect solution." She leaned forward and grabbed my hand. "As are you, Rowan. We felt a little guilty leaving the earth to the whims of the Titans, so we chose you as the Greek Dragon God. Our champion, in the spirit of old."

I nodded, carefully slipping my hand free of hers. Fantastic. She wanted me to fight a battle that even the gods themselves felt was too dangerous.

Just our luck.

"And really," she added. "It's a huge deal that I would leave here to take the Titans' souls to Tartarus. So you should be grateful."

"I am. Of course. Thank you. And I'll do my best." There was nothing else I could say, really. This was not a woman who was going to budge from her beach house or her hobbies. "Is there anything else you can tell us about finding the vessel?"

"I'll transport you to a place that is nearby. Search for the Cave of Treasure by following the setting sun. It will be a dangerous journey, meant to test your mettle, but that's the only kind of journey worth taking."

Easy for her to say. It looked like the only journey she took these days was to the yoga studio and juice bar.

"And Rowan," Hera added. "When you face the Titans, you'll need to be strong. They're going to hit you with something you won't expect. Something that will test your mettle in ways you've never been tested. Fight it. With all your might, fight it."

I nodded, about to open my mouth to ask more questions. Did she mean the darkness that the dragons had mentioned?

Before I could ask, she waved her hands. "Now go, the lot of you. There's a treasure you must find, and you don't have much time."

Magic pulled at me, the ether sucking me into a massive portal that Hera had created in her kitchen. I gasped as it yanked me through space, spinning me around until my head buzzed.

When I appeared on a rocky stretch of ground, I staggered, nearly going to my knees. Maximus grabbed me. He was wobbly himself, and we kept each other upright.

I panted, catching my breath, and turned to do a count. Bree and Ana stood next to each other, both of them windblown and a bit woozy-looking. Cade and Lachlan stood next to them, their feet planted widely as they got their bearings.

"Well, that was something," Ana said.

"She was a trip." Bree shook her head. "I'm not so sure about those girls' nights. I don't think I want to sit on her couches."

I chuckled and turned, taking in my surroundings in more detail. We stood on a strange flat plain that was dotted with odd stone sculptures. They looked as if they'd been carved by thousands of years of wind and rain. Most of the sculptures were about my size, but they weren't shaped like humans. They were more abstract than that.

In the distance, the sound of waves crashed against the shore. I turned toward it, spotting a gray sea that broke against the beach. A massive gray sea monster leapt into the air and splashed down into the water with the force of a train going off a bridge. I'd only had a moment to catch sight of its fangs, but it was enough to be sure I didn't want to go in that direction.

Fortunately, the sun was setting in the other direction. I turned toward it. "Ready?"

"Let's get this over with," Ana said. "This place gives me the creeps."

She was right. There was something in the air here that was really unpleasant. Dark magic, yes. But something else.

We began to walk, following the sun as we cut between the rock formations that silently guarded the desert that seemed empty of life.

"I'm going to try to figure out how far away we are." Bree's wings flared from her back, and she leapt into the air.

Her silver feathers glinted in the sun, and she did a quick circle overhead, checking out our surroundings. She landed gracefully next to us.

"I didn't spot any caves, but there are some strange shadows moving on the ground." Worry creased her brow.

I nodded. "We'll keep an eye out."

We continued walking, and I kept my senses alert. If something was going to sneak up on us, I wanted to know about it. Thank fates for Artemis's gift.

Maximus kept close to me, his gaze wary on the surroundings. Everyone in the group was tense as we walked, waiting for an attack that felt inevitable.

When I first heard the growling, it was so quiet that I wondered if I was imagining something.

But then it came louder.

"You hear that?" Bree asked.

She also had super hearing, a gift from the Norse god Heimdall.

"I do. Coming from the left."

We kept moving, but everyone trained their gazes on the left. When the wolves appeared, I stiffened.

"I think we've identified the gray shadows," Bree said.

There were at least forty of them, a massive group. They were big, too—each of them at least six feet long. Their fur was a rough gray-brown, and it stood up at their hackles. Their lips were pulled back from sharp fangs, and they lowered themselves in an attack stance.

Oh fates. This is bad.

12

The wolves crouched low, their growls filling the air as they crept closer.

"Crap!" I called upon Artemis's magic, thrusting it toward them. I worked mostly on instinct, hurling the power out of me. "No one draw any weapons. Not yet. We don't want them thinking we are a threat."

Ana joined me. She, too, had a gift with animals, though hers wasn't quite the same as mine. She could calm them, though, and I felt her magic flowing on the air, moving toward them. Sweat dripped down my spine as I watched them, my muscles trembling.

The wolves only relaxed slightly. Their growls softened, but their lips stayed pulled back from their fangs as they snarled.

Next to me, magic swirled around Cade. It smelled of a storm at sea and tasted of tart apples. A moment later, a massive wolf stood in his place. He dwarfed the other wolves, standing at least twice as tall.

Their gazes darted over him, confused at first.

I pushed my magic toward them, trying to calm them. Ana did the same, and slowly, their growls softened. They never looked away from Cade, though, who maintained an alpha's stance. His snarl was even fiercer than theirs.

Finally, the wolves lowered their heads, signs of submission toward Cade.

"They've chosen him as their alpha," Maximus said.

"Well, they'll be disappointed, because he's coming home with me." Bree grinned. "But good work, hon."

Cade growled at a different pitch, and it sounded like an acknowledgment of Bree's words.

"Now what?" Ana asked.

I thought of the little cat who had given me directions before. "I'm going to try to ask them where to go."

"Like we're stopping at a gas station, and they're the clerk who's going to tell us how to get to Poughkeepsie?" Bree asked.

"Like that, but hairier." I looked at the wolves, keeping my voice low. "Can you tell us how to get to the Cave of Treasures? Are there any shortcuts to take or dangers to avoid?"

The wolves kept their heads down, eyes glued to Cade. They didn't answer me. I tried asking telepathically, sending my question along with my magic toward the biggest wolf. I had to imagine that the former alpha was a bit annoyed at the idea of being replaced. Maybe he'd help us go on our merry way.

Unfortunately, he told me nothing. There was one moment when I thought this would work, then it passed.

Dang.

"Okay, I'm getting nothing." I frowned.

Cade stopped growling, then twitched his head toward the right. It was a clear gesture that we should get moving. I looked at Bree for confirmation, and she nodded.

I hated the idea of retreating—of showing my backs to the wolves—but Cade had it under control. And no way he'd let the wolves come after us.

As a group, we turned and left Cade, walking slowly away.

Bree kept her gaze on her man, a frown beginning to crease her face. I could tell she was about to stop when Cade finally trotted away from the wolves.

They rose to their full height, watching him leave. My heart set up a rhythm in my chest, and it only relaxed when I realized that the wolves were definitely not following and that Cade's face looked calm.

He joined us, then took the lead. We followed, and I felt like I was in an episode of some nature show narrated by David Attenborough.

I did my best impression of his voice and murmured, "And the herd of frightened humans follows the noble wolf through the creepy desert."

Next to me, Maximus chuckled.

I chanced a look back at the wolves, and they were trotting away in the other direction. Once they were fully out of sight, Cade shifted back to his human form.

Bree pressed a quick kiss to his lips. "So, what was that all about?"

"We just came to a friendly agreement," Cade said. "Which wouldn't have been possible without Ana and Rowan's magic calming them down." He shook his head. "They were *moody*."

"Well done, man." Lachlan clapped him on the back. "I didn't fancy a fight with that lot."

"Neither did I." Cade ginned. "And I did get them to tell us where to find help and a shortcut."

"Really?" Excitement flared in my chest.

"Aye. They understood your question, but they directed the answer to me. There is a settlement just over that rise there." He pointed to a sloping hill with a few of the weird stone statues on it. "We should be able to find some skinny people to help us."

"Skinny?" I frowned

"That's what they said."

I grinned at him. "All right, then. Let's get a move on."

We set off toward the hill, and I hoped these skinny people had a really fast shortcut. Their settlement was a bit out of the way, but it would be worth it if they could shave off a bit of the journey. It didn't take long to crest the rise, and I spotted the small settlement in the valley below.

The houses were built of the rough stone that scattered the plains here, and a fire burned in the middle of the camp. A strange assortment of feathered things sat at one side of the settlement. They were about the size of cars. Bigger, actually.

I squinted harder at them. "What are those?"

"No idea," Bree said.

No one else could see them closely enough to fugue it out, either.

We hurried down toward the main gate that led into the settlement. We were still about twenty yards away when the gate opened and a dozen slender people filed out. They really were skinny. So skinny that they looked like they were mostly bones. Their faces were different, too, with smaller eyes and thin lips. Pale blue hair flowed from their heads, matching the simple tunics they wore.

Though they were shaped vaguely like humans, they definitely weren't. Though they were skinny, it didn't look like a starvation situation. They all looked healthy with bright eyes, shiny hair, and beautiful clothing, and three of them were idly chewing on some kind of fruit.

"Who dares trespass on our land?" asked the one who led the group. He was the tallest of all, nearly seven feet, though he couldn't have weighed more than a hundred and twenty pounds.

"I am Rowan Blackwood. I was sent by Hera to find the Cave of Treasures." I gestured to my companions, but before I could say their names, the man spat on the ground.

"Hera." He scowled.

"I know," I said. "She's, um, a character."

He seemed to get what I meant and nodded in a satisfied manner. It was good, since I wouldn't dare insult the goddess. But since this guy clearly appreciated a little shit talking, I was glad he was able to interpret the meaning behind my words.

"Why are you here?" he asked.

"The wolves told us that you could help us."

"The wolves." He spat again.

Fantastic, he liked no one.

"Could you help us?" Maximus asked. "We're happy to pay you."

"Payment." He scoffed, and I'd never heard such disgust in a single sound. "We are the Eleri, and we serve only the dragons. Your money cannot buy us."

"The dragons?" I asked, looking to the skies.

"They've been gone many years, but we maintain our religion." The entire group bowed their heads.

"You worship dragons?" Bree asked.

The man nodded.

My mind raced. He wouldn't take payment, but he worshiped dragons.

Oh fates, could I do it?

Bree and Ana both looked at me, their brows raised.

I had to try.

I sucked in a deep breath and called upon the magic within me. It flickered through my muscles, faint. I tried again, envisioning my transformation. The magic sparked brighter, and my muscles began to ache.

Then I began to grow. My head rose, zooming up high above the settlement fence. The people in front of me gasped and fell to their knees, awe on their faces.

Oh, wow. No wonder the gods liked being worshiped.

I didn't want this kind of attention all the time, but if my self-esteem was ever a bit down, this wasn't the worst.

Soon, I stood towering over them. I looked down at my feet, spotting the pale silver scales and my metallic-colored claws. *Not bad.* I was really a good-looking dragon.

But now what?

My friends were staring at me with awe, and the skinny people below were still bowed low over the ground. I shifted on my feet, wondering if I should try flying to impress them even more.

My memory of my previous flying pulled me up short, though. That wouldn't impress anyone.

So I tried for some fire. At first, it was an unimpressive little blast of smoke.

Come on!

I needed this to work. Not just for right now, but for when I faced the Titans. I didn't have a lot of time to practice, and now was as good a time as any.

Again, I tried, feeling the burn in my chest. It rose up through my throat, and excitement thrummed along my nerve endings. Finally, a blast of fire puffed from my lips.

I nearly jumped with excitement.

The Eleri definitely did. They leapt to their feet and began to dance below me, their hands waving toward the flame.

"More!" they cried.

Uh, okay.

I tried again, blasting the flame above their heads. The fire was even bigger now, and the people shrieked their joy.

"Lower!" they cried.

I wasn't sure they worshiped dragons so much as they worshiped dragon fire. But I did as they asked, blowing the flame a little closer to them.

"Lower!"

I blew it a little closer. One of them leapt up into the air, high enough that his fingertips brushed the red flame. Instead of shrieking in agony, he howled with delight. His form glowed a bright gold, as if he'd absorbed some magic from my fire.

The rest tried to jump that high, too, but they couldn't manage it. I blew the fire a little lower, and they leapt into it, crowing with joy.

Okay, this was odd, but who was I to tell them what to enjoy?

Finally, I felt like I was nearly tapped out. It wasn't easy to be a dragon. It was a huge drain on my magical resources. I stopped blowing flame and shifted back into my human self, my head spinning as I shrank quickly.

The people blinked at me, their forms still glowing golden from my fire.

"You're human." The leader blinked again.

"Not exactly," I said. Actually, I was human. But he sounded so disappointed that I didn't want to confirm it. Honestly, it was almost as if he'd forgotten that I'd been a human to start with. The excitement of seeing the dragon had wiped it from their memories.

"We need your help," I reminded him.

He nodded, his gaze still traveling over me, confused and disappointed.

"We're going to the Cave of Treasures," I prodded.

His eyes brightened at that, as if he recognized it. "Yes. We can help you. If the dragon comes back and gifts us with more fire."

"Okay, but help us first," I said.

He nodded, then gestured for us to follow. "Come, come."

I shared a glance with my friends, who nodded. We followed the group of strange people into their settlement. The houses were more sophisticated up close, but it was the strange feathered contraptions that caught my eye. They sat at the other side of the compound.

If I wasn't mistaken, they were simple flying devices. The wings were covered in actual feathers, and each had two seats with pedals in front. The propeller in the back was connected to the pedals.

We followed the group toward them and stopped in front of the closest one.

The leader walked up to it, looking at us suspiciously. Finally, he stopped next to it and gestured at the wings. "We use these to fly over the Darklands. It is safer." He fiddled with the feathers. "The feathers make it appear to be one of the local birds, so they do not attack. They will accept you as one of their own."

The leader paused again—an unusually long pause—and inspected us. He seemed to be looking for a hint of the dragon that I'd turned into and was disappointed not to see it.

I shifted uncomfortably. It felt like this guy might go back on his word at any time.

"Clever." Maximus approached the flying device and walked around it, getting a good look. He ducked low to look underneath, and paid special attention to the props and gears.

"You will make it safely across as long as the Giant Monster doesn't appear."

"Giant Monster?" I asked. That was really generic. "What kind of monster?"

"The flying kind."

Okay, not great. "This is really the fastest and safest way?"

He nodded quickly. "Much faster and safer than the ground."

"We won't be too heavy for the machines?" Maximus asked.

The leader shook his head, his pale blue hair flying. "No. We are heavier than we appear. Very dense bones."

We'd have to take his word on it. "Okay, then. We'd like to take three machines if we could."

"First, the fire." The leader's gaze hardened.

"Okay." Crap. The pressure was on.

I closed my eyes and focused on the fire within me. It represented the dragon, and soon, my muscles ached. I grew tall, my head shooting up high. I looked down on the worshipers, whose eyes glowed with a fanatic light.

They waved their hands high.

I called upon the fire, feeling it rise in my chest. This time, I'd give them just a little poof of it. Not much.

I sucked in a breath, then expelled it, expecting to see a little burst of flame shoot from my lips.

It didn't.

Instead, an enormous jet of fire exploded from me. It was huge—almost the size of a house. It enveloped the people, who shrieked with joy. It *also* lit the closest flying machine on fire. Maximus lunged out of the way, barely avoiding certain death. The feathers on the flying machines went up like kindling, creating a bonfire that spread to the other five machines.

Within seconds, the entire fleet was aflame. The worshipers ran into the fire, darting around like kids on Christmas morning.

Horror opened a hole within my chest.

I stared at the inferno around me, then looked down at my friends. Their faces were white as they stared at the flames, shock dropping their jaws.

I tried to speak, to say "let's get out of here," but another little bit of flame burst from my lips.

As if she'd read my mind, Bree said, "Run for it."

We turned and sprinted away from the inferno, leaving the worshipers still shrieking with delight. My friends were fast and graceful as they ran through the settlement. I thundered along after them, trying to keep my tail from slamming into any of the buildings. I also made sure to keep my lips zipped up tight.

Since the gate was far too small for me to fit through, I decided to jump it. Of course my tail caught it on the downswing, and I dragged the gate down with me, like some drunken partygoer tipping over the red velvet ropes at the club.

Together, we ran from the settlement, sprinting back up over the hill. Finally, we stopped. I panted, directing my face away from anyone who I could possibly light on fire.

Once I'd caught my breath, I shifted back to human. I sat on the ground, exhausted and feeling much smaller in this form. Everyone else sat around me, staring.

"Sorry about that." I tilted my head back to stare at the sky. "What a disaster."

"It's just the learning curve," Ana said.

"Did *you* have such a big learning curve?" I asked, knowing that she hadn't. Bree hadn't either.

"No, but you're a freaking *dragon*."

"It's literally the coolest animal there is," Bree said. "If you got it easy, I'd be so consumed with jealousy I'd spontaneously combust."

I chuckled, looking away from the sky to meet their eyes. "I don't have a lot more time to practice."

"You'll get there," Maximus said.

"Speaking of getting there," Cade said. "We need to keep moving. With the shortcut gone, we need to pick up the pace."

I nodded, feeling even guiltier than I had been.

He held out his hands. "Don't feel bad, Rowan. Seriously."

"Yeah," Maximus said. "Especially since I can conjure some machines anyway."

My heart leapt. "Really?"

"Really. I got a good look at them. I didn't like that leader guy.

He was too suspicious. I don't think he was ever going to let us take those machines."

"Maybe not." I shook my head. "He knew I wasn't a real dragon."

"He liked your fire fine enough," Lachlan said.

"Let's get out of here before they're out of their stupor." Maximus stood, raising his hands. His face creased in concentration as the scent of cedar filled my nose and the taste of fine whiskey exploded over my tongue. Magic swirled in the air, and a moment later, one of the flying machines stood in front of us. "I sure hope it has all the right parts."

I chuckled.

"We'll only need two," Bree said. "Ana and I can fly alongside."

"What about the birds that we're supposed to be camouflaged from?" I asked.

"I'll make us invisible with my illusion," she said.

"Good plan." Maximus conjured one more. But he didn't stop there. He made another three as well.

"What are those for?" I asked.

"To replace the ones we ruined," he said.

"You mean, *I* ruined."

"Semantics." He grinned and pulled me forward, pressing a quick kiss to my lips.

"Well, thanks. That's nice."

"They're weird, but they probably need those flying machines."

"Yeah." I pulled back from him and approached one of the machines.

The steering mechanism was in front of the back seat, which sat slightly higher than the front so the pilot could have a good view.

Since Maximus had conjured these, he should get to drive.

As I saddled up in the front, Ana adopted her crow form. She was huge, with gleaming black feathers and onyx eyes. Bree's silver wings flared from her back, and she gave me the thumbs-up.

Maximus got in behind me, and Cade and Lachlan mounted their machine.

I fitted my feet into the pedals in front of me, then turned back to Lachlan. "Lift off in three, two, one..."

We began to pedal, and I gave it my all, pumping hard as the wheels began to rumble across the dusty ground. A shout from behind us had me turning my head, and I spotted the settlers running toward us over the hill. Their faces were no longer woozy with joy from the fire. They looked pissed as hell.

"Time to take off!" I shouted.

"Nearly there," Maximus said.

Next to us, Cade and Lachlan's machine lifted off the ground. Bree and Ana already flew overhead. We finally left the earth, the machine wobbling as it took flight. I looked down at the settlers, who were screaming after us.

At least they'd have the three machines that Maximus made for them.

It wasn't long before we'd left them behind. Their shouts faded in the distance, and all I could hear was the faint whistle of the wind as we soared over the world below.

Maximus turned us to face into the setting sun, and I squinted at the ground as we flew, searching for the cave. The guys were at our left, while Ana and Bree flanked our right. After a while, Ana moved to the other side to go alongside the guys. A moment later, she and Bree disappeared.

I touched my comms charm. "You still there?"

"Yep, right alongside." Bree's voice echoed out of the charm. "Figured it was time to go invisible in case the other birds showed up."

About twenty minutes later, they did. At first, they appeared as black specks on the horizon. Within five minutes, they were nearly to us. Their feathers were the same gray-brown as our machines, and they were enormous.

A happy laugh escaped my lips as they lined up alongside us, making us part of their flock. I stared at the one closest, taking in the keen gray eyes and the dark beak. It glided on the wind, so elegant and swift that it looked like magic.

My legs were aching but my heart was light. Every few minutes, Bree and Ana would check in. Bree would use the comms charm, while Ana would give a crow's caw. The last thing we needed to do was lose them while they were invisible.

When a horrific screech tore through the air, I nearly jumped out of my seat. I grabbed the bars on either side of me and clung to them, my heart thundering.

The birds around us peeled off, racing away.

Oh no.

They were fleeing.

I craned my neck, searching for the source of the noise. Sweat dampened my palms, and I spotted a massive black monster flying right for us. It was some combination of a bird and a bat and a lizard—and about four times as large as our machines. Its beak was big enough to chomp our little plane in half.

13

"I've got this," Bree's voice echoed through the comms charm.

"Be careful!" Cade shouted.

Ana cawed, and I knew she was going on the attack as well.

As the monster bird approached, I cringed at the sight of it. Up close, it was even bigger than I'd expected. It flew alongside us, and I debated grabbing a potion bomb to throw at it. I was blocked by my plane though, without a free shot. I could throw from the front, but we weren't facing the bird.

I couldn't see Bree as she approached the huge monster, and it made it even worse. Sweat dripped down my back as I watched, pedaling as hard as I could to get away from it.

Thunder boomed and lightning cracked, shooting straight down for the black bird as it neared us. The bolt plowed into the creature's back, and it shrieked in rage. Its eyes lit up like lanterns and its beak opened wide, but it didn't fall.

The bird didn't seem to like the lightning, but it didn't hurt it enough. Bree tried again, hitting the monster with another blast.

Again, the bird just shrieked its rage. It flew slower and more awkwardly, but it would take more lightning to send it to the ground.

The miserable creature reminded me of the Stryx—thank fates they were dead. I ignored my revulsion and tried out Artemis's power, opening up a line of communication with the bird that would hopefully calm it down and make it listen to reason.

As soon as I felt the bird's life force, it smacked into me like a sack full of bricks covered with spikes. I shuddered, dropping the connection immediately.

"I can't calm it down," I shouted.

The bird darted left, its beak snapping at the air. I couldn't see what it was attacking, but I could guess.

Horror chilled my soul as I screamed, "Bree!"

Her scream sounded then, echoing through the air instead of the comms charm.

"Drop the illusion!" Cade shouted. "He can smell you."

The illusion dropped, and I spotted Ana first. She was approaching the beast from the top, diving straight down. When I spotted Bree, I nearly died.

She was plummeting through the air, her wing broken. She'd dropped the illusion not because she'd wanted to, but because she was injured.

"Ana!" I screamed.

Ana seemed to spot the problem immediately and diverted her attention. She dived around the black bird and charged after Bree, who looked like she was falling faster and faster.

The bird stared after them, ready to attack.

Ana flew faster and faster, her powerful wings beating hard. She swept under Bree, catching her on her back and swooping away. A hazy grouping of clouds formed around them, obscuring them, and I realized that Lachlan was using his power over the weather to conceal them.

With Ana and Bree out of the picture, we could no longer try to escape. We needed to attack. As if they'd thought the same thing, Cade and Lachlan turned their flying machine to face the bird.

But they couldn't get too close. If they fell out of the air, who would catch them?

There was only one thing I could do.

I looked back at Maximus. His gaze caught on mine, just briefly, and he seemed to realize what I was thinking.

Dread filled his eyes. "Rowan."

"I have to." With that, I jumped out of the seat on the plane.

As the wind roared in my ears and my stomach leapt into my throat, I had one brief moment of abject fear.

Mistake.

I shoved the thought away.

Instead, I called on the dragon inside me. I had only seconds before I slammed into the ground. If I didn't shift—and fly—I was dead.

Fear pulsed through my veins, and the magic went to work inside me. Within moments, my muscles ached and the flame lit up inside my chest.

I'm shifting!

It was hard to tell when the transformation was complete, so I tried flapping my wings right away. At first, nothing happened. I looked back and realized they were super tiny.

Come on!

I imagined massive wings at my back, forcing my magic to surge toward that part of my body. My wings shot outward, expanding quickly. They glinted silver in the light of the setting sun, massive and majestic.

Hell yeah!

I might be an awkward teenager dragon, flopping my way through my growth spurt, but I was flying!

I swooped into the air, determined not to let my insecurity turn me back into a human. I had to fly and breathe fire and be the most badass dragon I could be. Not just for myself, but for my friends.

Cade and Lachlan had nearly collided with the giant black bird, and Maximus was following close behind. Cade, who sat in front, drew his silver shield from the ether. It was round, like Maximus's shield was, and he hurled it at the bird, taking advantage of the clear shot to be had through the front of the plane.

The silver glinted as it slammed into the bird's head. The beast tumbled through the air, thrown backward by the shield.

I hurtled toward it, determined not to let it clash with the flying machines. I moved fast, darting around the machines as I kept my gaze riveted to the monster. Flying became easier the more I practiced it, but I still felt like I might fall out of the sky at any moment.

Nope! Positive thoughts only!

I was a badass dragon!

I darted toward the giant monster bird, which had righted itself, and opened my mouth on a roar. The first blast of fire was a little bitty thing. The bird's dark eyes narrowed on it, almost like he was laughing.

Hell no. That wouldn't do.

I called upon the flame again, thinking of my friends. Fire exploded out of me, an enormous plume that enveloped the bird.

He shrieked, a sound of rage and fear, then flew in the other direction, tail feathers alight. The rest of his feathers looked charred as well, and he was out of sight in moments.

Holy fates, that had worked!

I turned back to the flying machines. All three guys were grinning at me. I grinned back—which probably looked insane when I was in my dragon form.

The levity lasted only half a second, however.

Bree and Ana.

I turned to look for them, spotting the faint misting of clouds that surrounded them. The clouds disappeared, and I saw Ana flying low toward the ground. A speck of silver glinted on her back—Bree.

I raced after them, the flying machines following at my back. As quickly as I could, I cut through the air, swooping low toward the ground. Ana had landed in a valley, and I joined her, making a very undignified landing on my claws and then galloping toward them.

I returned to my human form, then sprinted the last few yards. Ana, still a crow, crouched low so that a semi-conscious Bree could clamber off her back. Bree's wing was bent at a crazy angle, and blood coated the thing.

"The bird got you good." I dug into my potion belt.

"Bastard." Bree sat heavily on the ground.

Ana shifted back to her human form and knelt at Bree's side. "Here, let me help."

"Take this, too." I shoved the little vial at Bree, who took it and slugged it back. She had some healing ability, but she looked like hell and was willing to accept help.

"Tastes awful." She glowered at me.

"I'll make it taste like a Witch's Delight next time," I said, referencing her favorite pink cocktail.

Her features relaxed as the healing potion went to work. Ana hovered her hands over the wound as well, using her healing light to give it a little extra boost toward recovery.

"Bree!" Cade's voice sounded from behind us, and I looked back to see that the two flying machines had landed and the guys were sprinting toward us.

Cade knelt at Bree's side and cupped her cheeks. "Are you all right?"

"Better now." Her gaze met mine and Ana's. "Thanks, guys."

"Bastard bird," Maximus muttered. "They don't normally have a fantastic sense of smell."

"That's what I was counting on." Bree scowled. "But that one did. He knew just where I was. Hit me on the first try."

"Well, you're okay now." Ana lowered her hands and grinned. "All better."

Bree looked at her wing and moved it, smiling. "Thanks."

She stood, and I joined her, every muscle aching.

We were in a weird valley. On one wall, there appeared to be at least a hundred cave openings, each covered by an enormous pile of rocks.

"I think we've reached our destination," Lachlan said.

"But which one is the Cave of Treasures?" Maximus asked.

It was impossible to tell. "I bet if you try to open the wrong one, something terrible will happen."

"No doubt." Maximus nodded. "This is a protection measure."

"So we just have to pick the right one the first time." Ana approached the wall of caves. It stretched for nearly a mile in either direction. There was even a second level of cave entrances above the first one, set slightly farther back in the valley wall.

"How will we do that?" Maximus asked.

"I'll try." Ana sucked in a deep breath, clearly preparing to use her gift of Druid prophecy.

I leaned toward Maximus. "If Ana asks the right questions, her gift of prophecy will sometimes give her the answer."

"Fingers crossed, then," he said.

Ana's magic swelled in the air as she worked, and finally, she pointed to a cave entrance about two hundred meters away. "I think it's that one."

"Good enough for me." I started toward it, my friends at my side.

Once we reached it, we stopped in front.

"That's at least a million pounds of rock," Lachlan said.

"Worse, it's attached to the earth below." Cade pointed.

He was right. It wasn't loose rubble piled up in front of the cave entrance. The ground here was made of solid rock, and it looked like a giant had shoved the rock up against the cave entrance when the stone was still molten. It had dried against the entrance as a craggy rock door, totally solid and totally immovable.

Except they hadn't seen us coming.

I looked at Ana, then at Lachlan. They both had the ability to move large pieces of earth, and it was going to take all their skill, I'd bet.

"We've got this," Ana said.

The two of them stepped forward and raised their hands. Their magic filled the air with different signatures. The ground beneath our feet rumbled. The stone peeled back from the entrance to the cave, scraping loudly against the ground as it moved. Sweat trickled down Ana's temple as she worked, and finally, the path was clear.

The mouth of the cave beckoned, a gaping black hole that was as inviting as it was threatening.

Lachlan and Ana dropped their hands, their magic fading.

"Nice work." Bree started toward the cave, and we followed.

At the entrance, we hesitated. I listened carefully, peering into the dark.

After a while, I looked at Bree. "I'm getting nothing."

"Same. Let's go."

We crept into the cave, entering a tunnel that was about thirty feet wide. Silently, we moved through it. Soon, the light from the entrance dissipated, and we were plunged into darkness.

I raised my lightstone ring. Bree and Ana did the same. The

glow from our three rings illuminated the space, and we continued on.

Minutes later, we reached a diversion in the path. Our tunnel split into eight, and we had to choose.

I looked at Ana.

She nodded her head and closed her eyes. Her magic swelled on the air, and a moment later, she pointed to one of the middle tunnels.

It was narrower than the one in which we stood, but it was still wide enough for all of us to walk side by side. We moved through it on silent feet. When a glow shined from up ahead, I killed the magic in my ring. Bree followed suit, and we crept through the darkness.

As we neared, the golden glow brightened, becoming almost blinding. I squinted and crept forward, gasping when I spotted the interior of a gigantic cave.

It was at least three hundred feet tall, and just as wide. The whole thing was chock-full of gold. Piles of gold coins, trunks full of jewelry. Ingots and bars and plates. It formed a labyrinth within, so much wealth that it nearly made me ill. There were even gemstones among the lot, sparkling with rainbow fire.

"How the hell did this get here?" I whispered.

"A thief," Maximus said. "Only a thief would hide their treasure like this."

"Or a dragon," Bree said.

"There are no dragons here," I murmured. Somehow, I knew I would feel it if there were. "But there might be a monster."

The air reeked of dark magic, and I breathed through my mouth to limit the stench.

"How the hell are we going to find what we're looking for in here?" Lachlan asked.

He had a point. This place was just so *full*.

I crept forward, entering the labyrinth that was a temple to wealth.

We slipped between the piles of gold, some of which towered far overhead. On instinct, I headed toward the center of the room.

When a voice rumbled through the space, I nearly jumped out of my skin.

"Who dares trespass among my treasures?" The voice vibrated with such evil that I shivered.

I kept my mouth shut and kept moving forward, hoping to find the vessel before I found whoever spoke.

No luck, though.

"I see you amongst the piles of coins. You've come to steal what's mine!" He sounded immensely offended at the very idea.

Since we were currently standing amid massive piles of coins, I had to assume that he could see us.

"This can't be all your treasure. No single person could own this much," I shouted.

"Of course it's mine!" the voice boomed. "I killed all the previous owners, which means it's mine."

Killed?

Yikes.

A murderous thief.

I stepped out from between the coins, entering an open space in the cavern. My friends followed, spreading out behind me.

In the middle of the space sat a pedestal. Upon it, a small golden vase sat in a place of honor. Something inside my chest pinged with awareness.

That's what we were after. Small and unassuming—at least amongst everything else that was here—but capable of holding the souls of Titans.

A man stepped out from behind trunks that vomited up

pearls and diamonds. He had a ruddy complexion and black eyes that gleamed like a snake's. Green hair topped his head. The magic that rolled off of him was deep and evil.

"A goblin," Cade murmured.

"Goblin?" I asked.

"They hoard treasure."

"Indeed, we do," the goblin said. "And I'm sure you've something on your person that I could add to my collection after I've killed you."

"Hell no, we're not joining your collection," I said.

"Why not?" He pointed to the jewels that sat next to him. "That once belonged to a queen of Spain. Oh, how she screamed when I killed her. Wouldn't you like to join her?"

"No. And yuck." The gleam of excitement in his eyes really grossed me out.

"And then that over there..." He pointed to a collection of gleaming golden chairs. "They belonged to the Fae king of Anchromea. He was not very pleased when I cut off his—"

"Stop!" I held out my hands. "We don't need to know any more. You're a miserable bastard who has killed a whole lot of people to create this creepy collection. We get it."

"Creepy?" Anger flushed his face, turning it an even deeper red. "I'll show you creepy."

Magic swirled around him, dark and fierce. It swept him up in a tornado, no doubt turning him into something awful. Before he could finish the transformation, I darted toward the pedestal in the center of the open space.

I just had to grab the vase before he changed.

I was nearly there when the black tornado that surrounded him exploded in a blast. Something slammed into me, smacking me aside and throwing me up into the air. I flew high, and somehow—miraculously—Maximus caught me.

My heart thundered as I looked up at him, catching sight of an enormous tentacle smashing back down to the ground.

Oh, hell no.

Tentacles?

I squinted through the dark smoke that was dissipating and spotted a huge creature. He looked like a green land octopus, with at least ten legs and an enormous head sporting beady black eyes.

"The Goblin King," Cade muttered. "Just our luck."

"What's the Goblin King?" I asked as my gaze darted around the space, looking for a place to hide.

"Only the most dangerous goblin in existence. He lives for treasure, and the number of people he's killed is more than we can guess."

Maximus drew a sword from the ether, looking like a total bad ass. "Then let's take care of the bastard."

14

A t his words, a tentacle snapped toward us. It was as wide around as a car, and glinted a brilliant green. We all dived out of the way as it smashed down into the pile of gold behind us, sending the coins flying.

I slid into a crevice between two golden benches, covering my head. The coins pinged off of me, hurting like hell wherever they hit. Maximus slammed into the hiding space with me, trying to shield my body with his own as he kept his sword away from me.

Once the coins stopped flying, I jumped to my feet. I could turn into a dragon to fight this guy, but I was still nervous about my fire. It'd gone out of control last time. Better to try something safer to start. I drew a potion bomb from my bag. It was a hardcore stunner, but I had a feeling I'd need more than one.

The Goblin King rose high above us, at least twenty feet in the air, his tentacles stretched throughout the cavern, writhing over piles of gold as they searched us out.

At my side, Cade hurled his round shield at one of the tentacles. The shield flew straight, severing the tentacle in one smooth movement. Green blood sprayed, and the Goblin King shrieked.

While he was distracted by that, I chucked the potion bomb at his head. It smashed into his face, and he swayed, his eyes crossing. A moment later, he shook his head, his expression clearing, and managed to stay upright.

His enraged roar shook the chamber itself, causing piles of gold to shift all around.

I scrambled away from the pile that began to rain down, threatening to crush me, and skidded on the coins.

To my left, Maximus lunged for one of the tentacles that was about to slam down on my head. He stabbed it with his sword, then yanked the blade to the side, dragging the tentacle with it.

The tentacle must have been able to exert a thousand pounds of muscular force, but Maximus managed to pull it tight.

An idea flared, and I pulled my electric sword from the ether. The weapon crackled with energy as I sliced it toward the tentacle. It took a few bloody hacks to get all the way through the thing, but I managed.

The Goblin King roared again, and something heavy hit me in the back.

Another tentacle.

It lifted me up and flung me against the stone wall. I hit the side so hard that my body exploded with pain as I dropped to the ground.

Aching, I sat against the wall, blinking bleary eyes at the fight going down in front of me.

Lachlan had turned into an enormous black lion and was attacking the Goblin King's throat, leaving massive wounds in the surface of his flesh. Green blood poured down over the gold, but the Goblin King kept fighting.

Bree and Ana had adopted their flying forms. Ana was destroying one tentacle with her claws, while Bree was using her strength to tie two tentacles together. Maximus raced toward me, concern creasing his brow.

Despite the fact that the Goblin King was shaped like a giant octopus, he could still speak. "I'll kill you! I'll tear your guts out through your mouth and wear your heads as hats. You'll never know pain like the pain I'll deliver."

Honestly, given the aches that rolled through my body, I believed him. This guy was capable of a hell of a lot.

Maximus reached me and helped pull me to my feet. "Are you all right?"

"Yeah. Let's just finish this guy." Everything ached as I staggered toward the center of the cavern where the battle was going down.

The Goblin King still had four tentacles in operation, and he used one to smack away Lachlan, who was still tearing at his enormous throat with his claws and fangs. The black lion flew head over tail and slammed into the stone wall, just as I had done.

Rage boiled in my chest at the sight of my friend crumpled on the ground. The dragon within me burst to the surface. I hadn't called on it—not consciously—but suddenly, I was twenty feet tall and in possession of some serious claws and fangs. Any concern I'd had about the small space and my fire dwindled.

I could do this.

I *had* to do this.

I roared, a sound that shook the cavern itself. No smoke burst from my mouth, thank fates.

I took off into the air, my powerful wings carrying me high. As if they got the message, my friends cleared out, darting toward the edges of the cavern. I swooped low over the Goblin King, blasting him with a jet of fire that melted the gold beneath his body.

He shrieked, his tentacles waving.

That's probably what your other victims felt, you jerk.

I gave him one last enormous blast, wanting to end his misery and get this over with. The fire was so hot and so fierce that it turned his head to ashes in a second.

Wow, dragon fire was amazing.

The tentacles flopped to the ground, lifeless, and I whirled on the air, surveying the piles of gold to find my friends. One by one, they strode toward the middle of the cavern. Ana, now in her human form, was crouched by Lachlan. He'd also shifted back, and he was staggering to his feet. Everyone else looked fine, thank fates.

Satisfied that my friends were safe, I searched for the vessel. My gaze landed on it almost immediately, as if it called to my soul. It was half buried in a pile of coins, nearly impossible to see. If it hadn't called to me, I might have missed it entirely.

I swooped down and landed next to it, my tail smashing into a pile of coins and sending them sliding.

Whoops.

I'd have to be more careful with that thing.

I shifted back to human form and snagged the vessel quickly, turning to look at my friends. "Let's get the hell out of here."

Lachlan created a portal, and we were home within minutes. All I wanted was a shower and a nap, but as soon as I appeared on the castle lawn, I spotted the Centaurs and the Cyclopes.

"Looks like I can kiss that nap goodbye," I muttered.

"No kidding," Ana said.

The Amazons were there as well, clustered near the castle wall. Over a hundred of them, each dressed in their black battle clothes. I smiled, glad to see them but dreading the reason they were at the castle.

It was pure chaos there, with people running around, clearly prepping for battle. Most carried weapons or wore some kind of armor. A lot of it was modern tactical wear, though a few people were wearing more ancient stuff. To each their own.

"Something has changed," Maximus said.

Bree frowned. "The Titans must have made progress with the crystal. It looks like we're about to go to war."

My heart thundered, and I clutched the vessel tightly. Damn it, I wasn't ready yet. I had no idea how to get their souls into the vessel.

I searched the courtyard for Jude and spotted her striding toward us. She'd nearly reached us when I blurted out, "Is it time?"

She nodded sharply. "Our recon at the Titans' fortress suggests that their spell is nearly complete. The golden crystal has been hooked up to the power source and is spinning faster than ever. Soon, they'll have converted the entire world to their dark magic—including us. There's no more time to wait."

"But I'm not ready. I don't know how to put their souls into the vessel." I held it up.

"You're going to have to figure it out on the spot, because we are literally out of time. Once we've converted to their side, there will be no one left to fight them. But if we can stop them now, we'll turn back the damage they've done. Now that you're here, we can go."

Something loud clanged in my head as my mind raced, searching for a way to get their souls into this vessel. I had *no* idea, unfortunately. Just...nothing.

Jude met the gazes of everyone in our group. "We've found a weakness in their fortress wall, and our army is ready. I was hoping that you could take your buggy and get close enough to the wall to deploy the bombs that Hedy made. Once we have an entrance into their fortress, the entire army will approach."

Bree nodded, and I heard her speak through the buzzing in my head. "Of course, the buggy can be ready to go in minutes."

"Good. The Cyclopes and Centaurs have agreed to provide cover for your approach."

Heck yeah, that would definitely help.

"You all look like hell," Jude said. "Go get a power-up potion from Hedy. It should give you some energy."

More magical speed. But we didn't have a choice. I was so exhausted that I was dragging like a new mother with a colicky infant. I nodded at Jude, hoping that Hedy's potion would clear up my mind and give me a genius idea about how to get the Titans into the vessel.

As if she could read the concern in my eyes, Jude reached for my hand and squeezed. "You can do this, Rowan. I have faith in you. And even if you need some extra time to figure out how to get their souls into the vessel, perhaps we can contain them long enough to give you that time. We've got a pretty impressive force here."

I looked around, taking in even more people than before. Allies were still arriving, and she was right. This was an incredible army. I spotted the FireSouls by the castle doors. Nix, Del, and Cass stood with their guys, Ares, Roarke, and Aiden. Mordaca and Aerdeca stood with them, each kitted out entirely in black and white respectively. Gone were the Elvira dress and white pantsuit, however, and in their places were tactical outfits in their signature colors.

They waved but didn't smile. Nix, Cass, and Dell waved with big grins on their faces, and I knew they were excited to get into a fight. They loved a good fight.

"And there's some good news," Jude said. "You know the troops outside the castle walls?"

"How could I forget?" They were literally here for me.

"We found a way to trap them here, so we won't have to fight them at the Titans' fortress. And once the Titans are dead, their magical sway over the humans will disappear. That leaves just the demons to deal with. Easy peasy."

I smiled at her, genuinely happy. It meant less death and injury for all, and I could definitely get behind that.

"Be ready," Jude said. "We leave in ten."

With that, she turned and walked away. My shoulders slumped.

Maximus laid a heavy, comforting hand on my shoulder. "Don't worry, Rowan. You've got this."

I nodded.

"Yeah, you've got it," Ana added. "No question."

"I have faith in you." Bree gave me a quick hug, then stepped back. "I'm off to prep the buggy. Snag me a power-up potion from Hedy."

I saluted her. "Will do."

She ran off to the buggy, and the rest of us headed into the castle. On the way in, I spotted Connor and Claire, my other friends from Magic's Bend. They waved, their expressions serious. Connor had a bag strapped over his shoulder that looked just like mine. No doubt it was filled with potions. Claire wore her fighting leathers with her hair pulled back, and she gripped her sword loosely in her hand.

There were so many people flowing out of the castle that we climbed the stairs into the main entryway like salmon going upstream. Once inside, Maximus stopped me.

"Really, Rowan. You can do this. You'll find a way." His expression was serious, as if he were trying to force some of his faith into me.

I smiled up at him, wishing I believed him.

"He's not wrong, you know." The voice came from behind me, vibrating with power.

My heart thundered as I turned, spotting Arach, the dragon spirit who guarded the castle. She appeared in her human form, which looked a bit like a transparent blue ghost. Her features were beautiful but reptilian. Hundreds of years ago, she'd given her magic and her life to create the Protectorate, and now she guarded it. I was rarely granted an audience with her. No one was.

Her power was so immense that it made me lightheaded to stand near her.

"Arach." The words came out as a squeak.

"Rowan Blackwood. You have done well."

"Thanks." Warmth glowed in my chest at her words, but not for long. "Except I have no idea how I'm supposed to get the Titans' souls into the vessel."

She reached out and laid her hand on my arm. I couldn't feel the warmth or solidity of her form since she didn't have one, but her magic flowed through me, bolstering me. "You will find a way. When the time comes, the answer will come to you as well. It is inside of you. Have faith, Rowan. You can make the final choice. Only you."

I nodded, wishing that she had more explicit instructions but willing to take what I could get. "Thank you, Arach."

With that, she disappeared.

I was still scared silly, but I felt a bit better.

Maximus squeezed my hand. "Let's go find Hedy."

Once Maximus and I had collected power-up potions and the bombs from Hedy, we returned to the front lawn. The troops were all gathered in groups, ready to be transported to the field of battle. Lachlan walked amongst them, along with Emily, the transport mage. Between the two of them, they'd create enough portals so we could get our army there.

Then all we had left to do was defeat the Titans.

As Jude would say, easy peasy.

Not.

I shook away the negative thoughts and strode toward Bree and the buggy. Our fighting machine looked as good as ever. We'd built the hulking car ourselves when we'd been teenagers, using spare parts and things we'd scavenged from car graveyards.

The result was something that looked like a Humvee with no top. The sides were covered in huge spikes that were coated in Ravener poison, and platforms were built over the hood and extending off the back.

Bree was already standing on the front fighting platform that was built right over the hood. Caro stood next to her, platinum hair gleaming. Ana sat behind the wheel, a bright smile on her face. No matter how dangerous the goal, Ana loved driving the buggy. Cade stood on the back fighting platform, his expression set.

I strode up to them, raising the power-up potions in the air. "I've got the stuff."

They grinned. The power-up potions were basically magical energy drinks, but super strong. We weren't supposed to take them often or they'd overload our system.

Maximus and I climbed into the buggy, and I handed out the potions. I slugged mine back, then joined Bree and Caro on the front platform, while Maximus took up position on the back platform with the rest of the guys.

Bree handed me a harness and grinned. "Safety first."

I strapped the harness around my waist and clipped it off to the front safety bar that wrapped around the platform at waist-high level. When we'd been teenagers on our first trip in the buggy, we'd learned the hard way that we needed safety harnesses.

All around, the groups of fighters whispered and readied themselves for battle. Portals gleamed in front of them, ready to be used to reach the site of battle. Between the Protectorate, the Order of the Magica, the Amazons, our friends from Magic's Bend, and the Greek mythical creatures, we had an army of at least two hundred.

Not bad.

Jude strode up to our buggy. Her electric whip was coiled at her side and her face was battle ready, set in serious lines. "Ready?"

"Ready," we all said in unison.

"You'll go first. Caro will lead you to the weak spot in the castle wall. Deploy the bombs, and once our entryway is established, join the fight."

"On it."

She smiled at us. "Good luck and be safe."

Lachlan strode up to us and stopped right in front of the buggy to make a large portal. Once it gleamed, ready for Ana to drive through, he climbed onto the back platform to join Cade.

"Go!" Jude shouted.

Our army began to flow through the portals, heading toward war. Ana hit the gas, and the buggy rumbled forward. I gripped the safety bar in front of me, my heart thundering.

The ether sucked us in, spinning us through space. I held my breath until we arrived, then gasped at the sight of the fortress.

I'd never seen it from this angle. Holy fates, it was big.

The structure was built of midnight stone and towered into the air. It was so huge that it looked like something from an alien planet. The fortress sat on an enormous stone mountain that sloped gradually upward. Lightning crashed in the dark sky, illuminating the golden crystal that spun with incredible speed.

Ana wasted no time in pressing her foot to the gas. I clung to the front railing of the buggy as it plowed forward, eating its way up the side of the mountain. Thunder boomed as lightning lit up the sky, making the fortress look haunted.

My heartbeat roared as we approached, a chill racing over my skin.

This was it—the battle that would determine our fate.

15

The Cyclopes and Centaurs thundered alongside us, ready to provide cover should we need it.

I was certain we would.

The wind blasted the hair back from my face, and I grinned, despite the fact that I was possibly racing toward death. Fear and joy combined, a strange mix. I'd always loved the buggy, and that was never going to change.

"Head toward the left side of the fortress," Caro shouted. "The weak spot is there."

Ana turned the wheel slightly left and zoomed toward our target. I looked back over my shoulder, spotting our army as it appeared through the portals. With every second, more people arrived, waiting to launch the attack.

I squinted up toward the fortress walls, looking for a sign of any guards. The golden crystal continued to spin, and as we neared it, something strange happened. It was almost as if I could feel the power of the crystal in my chest.

It was dark.

As dark as the magic that I'd shoved deep down inside me. It called to me, pulling on that dark magic, trying to drag it to the surface. I stiffened, gripping the railing tight, and looked away from the crystal.

Fight it.

As we neared the base of the castle, I swept my gaze over the top of the ramparts. I spotted the tiny figures right before the magic began to fly.

"Look out!" I shouted, just as a massive ball of fire hurtled toward us.

One of the Cyclopes—Arges, I thought it was—thundered forward, raising his shield and slamming it into the fireball. The flame ricocheted back toward the fortress. It smashed into the wall about halfway up, leaving a deep dent.

Chiron the Centaur galloped up to join Arges and raised his bow. The arrow that he nocked glowed a brilliant green, and he aimed with perfect precision, sending the emerald arrow sailing through the sky to land in the chest of the one who'd thrown the fireball.

"Wow, they're a great team," Bree said.

"Best backup you could hope for." Caro grinned.

Another blast of magic hurtled from the top of the fortress tower. It gleamed a bright blue. Sonic boom?

Steropes, the other Cyclopes that I'd met, ran to meet this one. His footsteps shook the ground beneath the buggy. He caught the blast of magic against his shield, slamming it away just like Arges had. The power of the magic sent him to his knees, but he staggered upright. One of Chiron's fellow Centaurs joined Steropes and fired an arrow at the one who'd thrown the sonic boom.

The figure had already ducked behind the black stone wall, but the green arrow pierced the barrier. I heard the faintest scream, and knew that the Centaur's magical arrow had found its mark.

The fortress's defensive assault came faster now. More and

more blasts of flame and sonic booms. The Cyclopes did a good job of deflecting most of it, while Ana's crazy driving took care of the rest. She dodged at least two fireballs and one sonic boom while the rest of us hung on for dear life.

The closer we got, the harder the crystal pulled on me. The darkness inside me was rising, nearly impossible to fight.

"Do you feel that?" I asked, the words nearly painful to speak.

"Feel what?" Bree asked.

"The crystal." I pointed to it.

"I don't." She frowned at me.

"There are records of more and more people falling to the darkness," Caro said. "Ever since they got the power source, they've converted people much more quickly. Maybe you're one of them."

I wanted to believe that I was just like everyone else. But I knew this was different. I'd been warned.

Fates, I hoped I had the strength to fight it.

"Nearly there!" Caro shouted. "Get your bombs!"

I dug out one of the bombs that Hedy had given us. They weren't too dissimilar from my potion bombs, though they looked more like grenades than Christmas ornaments filled with liquid. Each of us had one, and we lined up so that we could get a clear shot.

"See the white paint?" Caro shouted. "Aim for that!"

I spotted it a second later. Caro had drawn a white X on the bottom of the stone wall when she'd been here last, and no one in the fortress had realized. Hell, they probably didn't even realize there was a weak spot in the wall.

"On my count!" Caro raised her bomb.

I did the same.

"Three, two, one!"

We all hurled our bombs. One by one, they crashed

against the stone wall, exploding in a fiery green blast. As the smoke dissipated, I spotted the hole that led right into the Titans' fortress. It was at least twenty feet across and ten feet high.

I turned back to check out our army, which was now advancing. They sprinted up the side of the black mountain, Jude in the lead. She had one hand out in front of her, creating a massive shield. I'd never seen anything quite like it, and it was clearly taking up a lot of her power.

The guards on the wall shot fire and sonic booms at them, but they exploded against Jude's shield. The Cyclopes and Centaurs filled the space between the army and the fortress, intercepting as many of the blasts as they could. Each one surely weakened Jude, so I hoped they stopped them all.

Ana pulled the buggy to a stop about forty feet from the fortress entrance. It was big, but not big enough. At best, twenty of our fighters could squeeze through at one time. The first ones to enter would be slaughtered immediately by the larger army within.

I looked at Bree, and from the look on her face, I'd bet twenty bucks she was thinking the same thing I was.

"We need to clear the way for them," I shouted.

"We can fly over the castle walls and create a blockade."

"I can do it with my fire."

"I'm coming!" Ana shouted.

I looked back at her. She was turned toward the back platform. "One of you take the wheel!"

Maximus leapt off the platform and took the wheel from her.

"Don't enter yet!" I shouted. "You'll be outnumbered."

He nodded, expression grim. "We'll go pick up some of the army. The run up to the top can't be fun."

"Good." I gave him a hard look. "Enter only with the rest of them when Ana gives the command."

"I'll fly down in front of the entrance," Ana said. "Then you know you can enter."

Caro clung to the platform, her gaze on us. "Good luck in there."

I dug into my bag and grabbed the little golden vessel, then thrust it into Bree's hands. "In dragon form, I can't hold this. You'll have to have it ready for the Titans."

"When will that be?"

"I don't know. But when I figure it out, I'll fly in front of you and shriek. That'll be the signal to get ready."

"Works for me."

"Right now, I'm going to hold their army back with my flame. You and Ana check out that golden crystal. See if you can break it."

"On it," Bree said.

I gave a two-finger salute, then jumped off the buggy, shifting into my dragon form almost immediately. It was easier now. Probably because of the practice, but also because I didn't have a choice. No way I was going to fail now.

Bree and Ana were already in the sky, silver and black wings carrying them high. I launched myself off the ground, surging toward them. My wings were strong, and I joined them quickly. The castle wall loomed above us, and we flew up over it, getting our first good view into the fortress below.

The massive black stone walls surrounded an enormous inner courtyard, just as I remembered. Hundreds of fighters milled around inside, waiting at the hole in the fortress wall.

I could feel the power of the Titans, but they hadn't arrived yet. No doubt they would be here soon, ready to defend their horrible empire.

Bree and Ana broke way, flying higher to reach the golden crystal.

I swooped down, calling upon the fire that burned in my

chest. I hoped that none of these cult members were innocent people who'd been dragged in by the Titans' darkness. Hopefully not. The first people to fall had been the ones who wanted to.

And anyway, they would kill my friends if given half the chance.

I was nearly to them when I blasted my fire, sending an enormous streak at the group in front. They shrieked and fell back, creating a gap between them and the hole in the fortress wall.

I'd like to be able to sweep through and take out all the people in a massive burst of flame, but I could feel that I wasn't strong enough. I didn't have an endless stream of fire, and I'd need to save a bit of strength for the Titans.

I kept up my attack, clearing a path for my friends to enter the fortress in great enough numbers to mount a suitable defense.

My fire held steady as I flew over the crowd, holding them back. The screams of pain and fear were awful.

The darkness in my soul liked it—a lot.

But I didn't. The true me hated it, and I clung to that. No matter what, I couldn't lose myself to the darkness. It was difficult, though. The crystal tugged so hard at me that I felt like I could convert at any moment. But then I'd be on the wrong side.

I'm protecting my friends.

The thought was the only thing that kept me going.

Bree swooped down next to my head and screamed, "I can't get the golden crystal. It is protected by the Titans' magic."

Damn it.

The crystal's power still pulled at me, igniting the darkness within. I needed to take it out.

Finally, I'd created enough of an open space that our army

could approach. Ana must have realized and given the signal, because soon, they were pouring in.

I killed my fire so my friends wouldn't enter an inferno.

The buggy came first, driven by Maximus. Aerdeca and Mordaca rode on the front. Mordaca fired her bow at the enemy, her incredible aim taking out one after the other. Aerdeca leaped off the platform and sprinted into the crowd, her sword raised high.

Lachlan and Cade leapt off the back platform, shifting into their lion and wolf forms in midair. They jumped into the crowd of the enemy, claws and fangs tearing. Ali, Harris, and Caro sprang out of the buggy's back seat and sprinted toward the fight.

Within seconds, Nix sprinted through the entry and conjured a barricade of sand bags for Connor. He ducked behind it, then threw potion bombs so fast his arm looked like a blur. His aim was perfect, and he felled enemy after enemy.

His sister, Claire, was already in the thick of it, swinging her sword with such ferocity that she beheaded a six-foot tall demon without appearing to exert any effort at all. Del, in her blue phantom form, fought at her side. Her sword glowed a bright cobalt, and she turned corporeal just long enough to stab demons straight through the heart.

Two griffons swooped through the air, their enormous beaks aiming straight for demon heads. Their claws glinted in the fire-light, and their feathers gleamed a golden brown. Cass and her man, Aidan, no doubt. He was the Origin, the most powerful shifter in the world, and she could mimic anyone's magic. Turning into a deadly griffon seemed to be a smart use of the skill.

I looked for a pocket of demons to attack with my fire.

"Oh, shit! The Titans are here!" Bree shouted.

I glanced up, spotting the Titans arriving in the courtyard. They were enormous, towering over the crowd as they approached. Cronos wore his enormous golden crown, while Crius's horns shot toward the sky. Theia's eyes glowed with a golden light that sent shivers down my spine. She'd be shooting fire at my friends any moment now.

As if Ana had thought the same thing, she dived from the skies. Her black feathers camouflaged her well, and Theia didn't see her coming since she was attacking from right above. Ana clawed at one of Theia's eyes.

The Titaness shrieked, blood pouring down her face as she reached up to cup the destroyed organ.

One eye down, one to go.

Crius, the ram-horned god, raised his hand. Lightning shot from his fingertips, headed right for the buggy.

I tried to shriek a warning, but the only thing that came out was a roar. At the last moment, one of the Cyclopes soared through the air, clearly having jumped from the top of the tower wall. He slammed his shield against the lightning bolt, sending it ricocheting away.

The lightning crashed against the castle wall and left a massive dent.

Cronos searched the sky, his giant golden crown glinting beneath the flashes of lightning. His eyes caught on me, and they brightened with delight.

"Rowan!" His voice bellowed through the night. "You are here. Join us. Complete your destiny."

This was *way* different than the message he'd given me last time I was here. They didn't want to kill me at all. They wanted me on their side.

But why?

I struggled to think as the crystal pulled at me and the darkness welled inside me. There had to be something about me that would help them fulfill their goal. I must be the final part of their puzzle.

I roared at him, and he laughed.

"You feel the pull even now," he shouted. "Join us and complete the spell. It is your destiny."

Complete the spell?

Did he mean that I was the last part of the spell that would turn the whole world evil?

He did. I could read it in his eyes. That was why they wanted me here. The crystal continued to pull at me, so hard I thought I might lose control of myself. It whispered dark things in my mind—dark things that I should do. Like attack my friends.

No.

I had to take out the crystal.

I flew toward it, beating my wings as fast as I could. I didn't have much time—I needed to help my sisters with the Titans. But if I didn't destroy this thing, it was all over. I knew it in my soul. I would turn to darkness and join the Titans.

The closer I got to the crystal, the harder it pulled. The evil inside me roared to life. It felt like black tar, filling up my insides and polluting my mind. *Kill your friends.*

I shook my head, trying to drive off the terrible thoughts, but they came faster and harder. I was nearly to the crystal. I could do this.

I raised my talons, reaching for the glowing golden rock. I'd crush it.

As soon as I collided with it, a massive force propelled me backward. I tumbled in the air but finally righted myself. I tried again, and it shot me back a second time.

It was pure evil, and it felt like it was rejecting the goodness within me. Every time I got close to it, I felt the darkness envelope more of my soul. On my third approach, it overtook me entirely. Evil exploded through me.

Kill them. Join us.

The urge was so strong that I looked down toward my friends. I nearly fell out of the sky when I saw that my scaled feet were now black. I turned to look at my wings. They, too, were black.

I had changed. No longer was I a silver dragon. My scales were as black as a demon's heart.

More than anything, I wanted to join the Titans in their goal. I *needed* to join them. It was my rightful place.

Deep inside, a small voice screamed. Vaguely, I recognized it as my true self, telling me not to do this. But I didn't listen.

I turned and shot downward, heading for the battle. I was going to blast the Protectorate and the Amazons to hell with my fire. Heat rose inside me, and I let out an experimental blast.

The flame was black.

No!

I ignored the voice inside me and flew lower, searching for the members of the Protectorate. My gaze landed on Jude. Then on Hedy. Caro. Maximus.

No!

The voice inside me screamed louder. I ignored it.

Out of the corner of my eye, I caught sight of my sisters fighting. Crius's hand smashed into Bree, sending her hurtling through the air to slam against the castle wall.

No!

My soul ached at the sight of Bree. When Theia struck Ana, something snapped inside me.

What was I doing?

I couldn't attack my friends. This was evil. Pure evil.

And that wasn't me, no matter what was inside my soul.

You can make the final choice.

Arach's words echoed in my mind, blasting so loud that I

couldn't ignore them. I'd chosen good before, and I would do it again. No matter how hard it was, I could do it again.

I turned from the battle, flying back toward the crystal. It took everything in me not to fight with the Titans instead of against them. My scales were still black and I still felt like I was drowning in tar, but I raced for the crystal.

This time, when I clawed at it, the dark magic didn't repel me. It embraced me.

So I used it. I gripped the crystal in both of my claws and squeezed so hard that it shattered.

The darkness drained from my soul immediately, sinking back down inside of me. It was still there, but it was truly part of me—more than it ever had been before. I felt like I had control of it now. It was a tool I could use.

I could breathe again. I could *think* again.

And my scales were silver again.

The darkness had tried to overtake me, but I'd chosen light. I'd used the dark magic to destroy the crystal, and now it could no longer take over my mind, dragging the darkness out of my control.

I controlled the darkness within me, and I could use it to take out the Titans.

I roared, flame blasting from my mouth, and swooped toward Cronos, determined to turn his arm to ash so he couldn't throw a sonic boom. I shot a blast of fire at him, but he knocked it away.

Fates, how did he do that?

I tried again, and it lit his shirt on fire, but he didn't fall.

I'm more deadly in my black dragon form.

I knew what I had to do.

I called upon the darkness inside me, determined to control it. This time, it rose to the surface but didn't overpower me. With the crystal gone, I could focus. My scales turned black, and the fire that shot from my mouth was the color of ebony. This time, I managed to light his arm on fire. He howled and surged backward, clutching the flaming limb.

Unlike last time, I didn't feel the pull toward ultimate evil. I was the master of this magic. I drove Cronos back farther, blasting fire at his other arm. As I dived around Cronos, swooping through the air, I tried to figure out how to get his soul into the vessel.

I could burn him like this, but I couldn't move his soul with my fire. So what was I supposed to do?

All around, the battle raged.

Ana and Bree had recovered from being smacked out of the air and were battling the Titans again. Ana was still trying to get Theia's second eye, but the goddess was now shooting fire from it. Bree helped, distracting her by flying around Theia's head.

Crius raised his hand to shoot a blast of lightning, but Maximus flew from the tops of the castle ramparts. He kicked Crius in the face, sending the Titan spinning backward. Maximus grabbed onto his cloak and went down with him.

Holy fates, he was brave.

The battle raged below. I caught sight of Aerdeca and Mordaca again, both covered in blood as they fought like banshees. Connor, Claire, the FireSouls, and all my other friends were still fighting like mad, risking everything.

Jude fought at the edge of the crowd, her electric whip sending the enemy flying through the air. I caught sight of the Menacing Menagerie, their fur flashing as they took down an enormous red demon with a sword the length of my leg. Caro shot her water daggers, slicing through the enemy until they fell, while Ali and Haris possessed two huge demons and used their bodies to fight.

Queen Penthesilea and Queen Hippolyta led a troop of

Amazons. They were headed right for the Titans, clearly determined to take on the biggest threat.

They were all so *brave*. Every single one of them was risking their lives for the good of the world. They were the opposite of the Titans—light to dark. I felt it in a way I'd never felt it before —as if being in my dragon form gave me an extra sensitivity to it.

An idea flashed in my mind, and suddenly I *knew*.

I knew how to defeat them.

I needed to do something I'd never done before—I needed to combine the dark magic and the light.

As if she sensed that I'd figured out how to stop her, Theia screeched and shot a blast of fire at me. I swooped away, barely avoiding it. The second blast hit me in the tail, and I roared.

Finally, Ana clawed at Theia's second eye, giving me a moment to put my plan into action. Tail aching, heart thundering, I whirled on the wind, taking in the battle below.

I could feel the goodness of my friends. Their determination to embrace the light and do what was good. It was almost a physical thing inside of me. Like a glow. I would use it.

I called upon the goodness in my soul and transformed myself back into the silver dragon. Then I flew in front of Bree, letting her know with a shriek that it would soon be time to catch the Titans' souls. I began to fly in circles above the battle, trying to focus on every positive thing I could think of. My friends' bravery, sacrifice, hope, and goodness. I could feel it in them, my dragon power like a magnet for it.

I called upon the sun magic that I'd used against the Titans the first time, letting it fill my chest with a golden glow.

I'd always had the power within me. It just needed a little extra juice. As I flew circles around the battle, I collected it all. Goodness and light flowed from my friends like a golden glow, and I drank it all up.

Then I called upon the darkness within me, adding it to the

mix. It rose up in my chest like tar, but I had control of it now. Hopefully I had enough to take out the Titans. As I turned to dive for the Titans, I caught sight of my silvery black wing. Silver *and* black.

My final form.

I was dark and light, good and bad, and I would use it.

I shrieked and hurtled toward my enemy, determined to hit them with everything I had.

Crius spotted me first. He raised a hand and shot a bolt of lightning toward me. It was so big and I was so close that my life flashed before my eyes.

It will hit me.

There was no way I could dodge fast enough.

Out of the corner of my eye, I spotted Maximus, once again plunging down from the ramparts, his shield in his hand. It was apparently his signature move, and he'd spotted Crius, too. But Maximus was fast. So fast that he got between me and the lightning, taking the brunt of the hit.

The lightning smashed into him, making him roar with pain. He dropped from the sky and crashed into the ground, and horror opened a hole in my chest.

No!

Everything in me screamed to go to him, to make sure he was okay.

"No!" Bree screamed, as if she knew what I was thinking.

Ana's crow caw echoed behind it.

They both knew what I was thinking, and they knew I couldn't do it. This was it—my only chance to stop the Titans. I had to keep going—like my sisters would.

It took everything I had to ignore Maximus—I didn't even know if he was alive—and race toward the Titans.

I have to keep going.

The sun's power was so bright inside me that I felt like I

might explode. It was strengthened by everything that I'd taken from my friends. I needed more darkness, more of the deadly force that the black magic gave me. I used my fear and grief for Maximus to help it rise inside me.

On instinct, I sucked in a deep breath, then blasted the Titans with my fire.

This time, the blaze wasn't red or black. Instead, it was a bright gold that blazed with light. It enveloped the Titans, who shrieked and howled. All the goodness in the world—or a lot of it, at least—enveloped them, along with the firepower of my darkness that took them to their knees.

Bree flew behind them, the vessel in her hands. We were working on faith here, and I hoped that Hera was right.

I continued to blast them with the power of light and dark, giving it everything I had. A great roar filled the air, and the walls of the fortress trembled. An explosion burst from the Titans, sending me tumbling in the air.

I righted myself just in time to see them collapse. Three golden blurs flew through the air and collided with the vessel that Bree held out in front of her. She toppled backward, clutching the vessel to her chest.

The Titans lay still. Their army stopped fighting.

Holy fates.

I panted, staring at the Titans. They really were down. And Bree held the vessel that contained their souls.

I'd done it—using the light *and* the dark. As long as I controlled it, they were both tools I could use to help the world.

The short burst of victory was followed by pure terror.

Maximus.

I turned, racing toward him, my wings carrying me as fast as I could go. I shifted back to human right before I landed so I wouldn't crush anyone.

Ana knelt at Maximus's side. She'd transformed back to

human, and tears streaked down her face as she held her hands over Maximus's chest, sending her glowing light of life and healing into his body.

I knelt beside them, a sob tearing from my throat.

"I don't know if he's going to make it," Ana croaked.

I reached for him, pressing my hands to his chest. "Come on, Maximus. I love you."

Tears poured down my face as I looked between him and Ana. She was doing everything she could, and I couldn't have loved her more in that second. Until he was conscious enough to swallow a healing potion, she was my only hope.

When Maximus gasped, I thought my heart might explode.

He opened his eyes.

"Are you okay?" I demanded. I wanted to throw myself over him and hug him, but I didn't dare. There was no telling what was broken.

"Fine." He grunted and tried to sit. He barely made it an inch off the ground. "Sort of fine."

I laughed through the tears, and Ana collapsed backward. He looked at her. "Did you bring me back to life?"

"I don't know." She shook her head. "I couldn't tell if you were dead. I just started feeding my healing light into you."

I scrambled for the potions in my belt. Now that he was conscious and could drink them, I'd pour them all down his throat.

I started with one, though, since too many could be damaging. Finally, he was able to sit.

I pressed a kiss to his lips, tears pouring down my cheeks.

He groaned and pulled back. "It might be a while before I can walk again, but I'll be fine."

"Good." I squeezed his hand. "Thank you."

He gave a half shrug, as if to say, *What else was I going to do?*

I looked at him one last time, then stood. Our troops had

already rounded up the demons who hadn't been able to flee when the battle ended. The unlucky saps who didn't have transport powers or charms would be sent back to the underworld. Some of the humans looked pissed, while others looked a bit confused. There'd have to be some kind of trial with the Order of the Magica to figure out who deserved punishment and who didn't, but that wasn't my job, thank fates.

I turned to find Bree. She stood behind the bodies of the Titans with Hera, who was now dressed in pink leggings and a white top. Her same messy blonde bun sat on her head.

"Go to them," Maximus said. "I'll be fine."

"I'll watch out for him," Ana said.

I turned to her and hugged her hard, whispering in her ear, "Thank you."

"Of course."

I gave Maximus one last look, then walked toward Hera and Bree. Jude joined me, along with Queen Penthesilea and Queen Hippolyta.

"How are casualties?" I asked.

"Not bad, considering," Jude said. "There are some grievous injuries, but we lost no one. Not yet, at least."

I prayed those injuries wouldn't take them.

"Same," Queen Penthesilea said.

My shoulders sagged. "Oh, thank fates."

My gaze scanned the crowd as I walked through. Mordaca and Aerdeca were looting the bodies of the fallen enemies. The Menacing Menagerie were doing the same, while my other friends from Magic's Bend were all gathered in a circle, talking and tending to their wounds. Ali, Haris, and Caro were slumped against the exterior wall, looking like they'd gone through hell. They were able to give me weary smiles, at least.

I walked by the fallen bodies of the Titans and stopped in front of Hera and Bree.

Hera smiled at me. "You did it."

"Barely."

"That just makes the story better." She lifted the golden vase, which now pulsed with a dark light. "I'll put this in Tartarus. You can be assured they won't escape again. Especially since they no longer have bodies."

"Thank you."

Her gaze moved to the fallen Titans. "On second thought, I suggest burning."

"I can take care of that."

We shared a few more words, then Hera left.

I hugged Bree, collapsing against her. "What a day."

"What a year."

I laughed and pulled back. "I'm going to take care of the Titans' bodies, then let's grab a drink."

She nodded, and I turned, transforming into my truest self. I roared and took to the sky, determined to banish every last bit of the Titans forever.

EPILOGUE

Two days later, once everyone had slept for twenty-four hours straight and done some healing, we met at the Whiskey and Warlock. Jude was throwing us a party, and after the wringer we'd just been through, folks were ready to let down their hair.

Unfortunately, there were still people recovering from the battle. The infirmary was full, which was saying something. With the healing magic that the Protectorate had access to, people would normally be all better within hours.

Not after that fight, however. A dozen people had been so grievously injured that they'd almost died, and it'd taken some quick work on behalf of the healers on our team. My potions store was tapped out, as were Hedy's and Lachlan's and Connor's, and all the healers had worked their fingers to the bone.

I couldn't be more grateful for the outcome, however, and as we walked into the Whiskey and Warlock, the smile that spread across my face was so big it almost hurt.

Ana nudged Bree and me as we walked into the warmth and said, "Finally, we get to have that drink."

I'd always wanted to be able to sit with them after a job and have a celebratory drink, and she knew it. I'd helped them with stuff in the past, but for the first time, I felt like I'd really earned it. Like I was truly part of the team.

I smiled. "Can't wait."

The little side room where the Protectorate always met was more crowded than it had ever been. People jostled at the bar and huddled around the warm hearth. The thick beams on the ceiling hung low over the crowd, the dozens of copper cups that dangled from them glinting in the light of the fire.

Lachlan and Cade stood at the bar, but I had eyes only for Maximus, who sat in a wheelchair by the fire. He looked like one of those badass Paralympic athletes.

I nudged Bree. "Get me a beer, will you? Something interesting."

"Sure thing."

I pushed my way through the crowd toward Maximus. I wanted to plop down on his lap, but that wouldn't help the healing process any. He should be walking again in a couple weeks, and I didn't want to do anything to slow that down.

I leaned over and kissed him. "Looking good, handsome."

He smiled at me. "Not too bad yourself."

Ali vacated the chair next to Maximus and grinned at me, gesturing to the seat. "For the lady of the hour."

"The lady of the hour?"

His eyes widened as if he'd said something he shouldn't have. "Going to get a drink. Want one?" He disappeared before I could say no.

I sat and looked at Maximus. "That was strange."

"Very." A secret glinted in his eyes, I was sure of it. But before I could ask, he spoke. "So, I was thinking. I'd like to make this official." He gestured between us.

"Official?"

"Yeah. With the labels and the real dates and all."

A grin spread across my face. "I could totally go for that."

"Yeah?"

"Yeah."

"Well, good." He pulled me close for a kiss.

As soon as my lips touched his, my body melted. *This.* I could definitely do with a lot more of this. And now that the worst of the danger was out of the way, we could see where it went. I had a feeling it would be lasting a long, long time.

"Drinks!" Ana's voice cut through the haze in my mind, and I pulled back.

She handed me a beer, and I sipped it, nearly moaning at the fizzy happiness of some kind of India pale ale. "Thank you so much."

"Anytime." She held out her glass of sparkling pink champagne.

Bree mimicked her motion, holding out a pink martini that gave off glittery smoke.

We clinked our glasses together, and I was so happy I could have burst. I looked around at all of my friends and colleagues, trying to think of an appropriate toast. "To health and happiness."

"Health and happiness," Bree and Ana echoed back at me.

I sank back into my chair, spotting the Menacing Menagerie across the way. Sophie had given them little cans of soda, and they seemed happy as clams on their shared seat at the bar.

"I really couldn't have better friends," I said.

They were *all* here, too. The Amazons, the folks from Magic's Bend, and all of the Protectorate. Even Lavender had given me a grudging, "Well done."

"Everyone! I'd like to make an announcement." Jude's voice

carried through the crowd. I spotted her by the bar, standing on a chair so her head rose above the others. "Rowan, will you come up here?"

Heat flooded my cheeks, but I did as she asked, pushing my way through the press of people as my sisters cheered me on. Ali stood next to Jude and another empty chair. He gestured to it, indicating that I should climb on.

I did, not letting go of my beer. It was like my security blanket. Once I was standing next to Jude, I looked at her, confused.

Her gaze was on the audience as she started to speak. "This isn't just a party. It is also Rowan's early graduation from the Academy."

My heart leapt, and I almost dropped my beer. "Really?"

Jude shot me a quick glance out of the corner of her eye, along with a grin. "Really." Then she looked back at the crowd. "We've been through the wringer these last few weeks, fighting an evil bigger than any we've ever faced. We wouldn't have made it without every single one of you."

The crowd cheered, raising their glasses.

Once they settled down, Jude spoke again. "Rowan performed above and beyond the call of duty. Without a doubt, she's one of the most powerful Magica to ever grace our institution. With that in mind, I am proud to offer her a spot in the Paranormal Investigative Team, so that she can fight evil alongside her sisters."

Joy exploded within me, so much that I probably glowed like a lantern. I blinked back the tears and nodded. All I'd ever wanted since I'd arrived at the Protectorate was to join the PITs. I wanted to protect the world alongside my sisters and couldn't imagine anything better. I even liked the dumb acronym.

"Do you accept?" Jude asked.

"Yes!" I nearly shouted the word as my gaze traced over the crowd.

It landed on my sisters and Maximus, and I knew without a doubt, that this was the best day of my life.

THANK YOU FOR READING!

I hope you enjoyed reading this book as much as I enjoyed writing it. Reviews are *so* helpful to authors. I really appreciate all reviews, both positive and negative. If you want to leave one, you can do so on Amazon or GoodReads.

This is it for Rowan's series, but a new series will be coming in Spring 2019. Keep an eye out. Join my mailing list at www.linseyhall.com/subscribe to stay updated and to get a free ebook copy of *Death Valley Magic,* the story of the Dragon God's early adventures. Turn the page for an excerpt.

EXCERPT OF DEATH VALLEY MAGIC

Death Valley Junction
   Eight years before the events in Undercover Magic

Getting fired sucked. Especially when it was from a place as crappy as the Death's Door Saloon.

"Don't let the door hit you on the way out," my ex-boss said.

"Screw you, Don." I flipped him the bird and strode out into the sunlight that never gave Death Valley a break.

The door slammed behind me as I shoved on my sunglasses and stomped down the boardwalk with my hands stuffed in my pockets.

What was I going to tell my sisters? We *needed* this job.

There were roughly zero freaking jobs available in this postage stamp town, and I'd just given one up because I wouldn't let the old timers pinch me on the butt when I brought them their beer.

Good going, Ana.

I kicked the dust on the ground and quickened my pace toward home, wondering if Bree and Rowan had heard from Uncle Joe yet. He wasn't blood family—we had none of that left besides each other—but he was the closest thing to it and he'd been missing for three days.

Three days was a lifetime when you were crossing Death Valley. Uncle Joe made the perilous trip about once a month, delivering outlaws to Hider's Haven. It was a dangerous trip on the best of days. But he should have been back by now.

Worry tugged at me as I made the short walk home. Death Valley Junction was a nothing town in the middle of Death Valley, the only all-supernatural city for hundreds of miles. It looked like it was right out of the old west, with low-slung wooden buildings, swinging saloon doors, and boardwalks stretching along the dirt roads.

Our house was at the end of town, a ramshackle thing that had last been repaired in the 1950s. As usual, Bree and Rowan were outside, working on the buggy. The buggy was a monster truck, the type of vehicle used to cross the valley, and it was our pride and joy.

Bree's sturdy boots stuck out from underneath the front of the truck, and Rowan was at the side, painting Ravener poison onto the spikes that protruded from the doors.

"Hey, guys."

Rowan turned. Confusion flashed in her green eyes, and she shoved her black hair back from her cheek. "Oh hell. What happened?"

"Fired." I looked down. "Sorry."

Bree rolled out from under the car. Her dark hair glinted in the sun as she stood, and grease dotted her skin where it was revealed by the strappy brown leather top she wore. We all wore the same style, since it was suited to the climate.

She squinted up at me. "I told you that you should have left that job a long time ago."

"I know. But we needed the money to get the buggy up and running."

She shook her head. "Always the practical one."

"I'll take that as a compliment. Any word from Uncle Joe?"

"Nope." Bree flicked the little crystal she wore around her neck. "He still hasn't activated his panic charm, but he should have been home days ago."

Worry clutched in my stomach. "What if he's wounded and can't activate the charm?"

Months ago, we'd forced him to start wearing the charm. He'd refused initially, saying it didn't matter if we knew he was in trouble. It was too dangerous for us to cross the valley to get him.

But that meant just leaving him. And that was crap, obviously.

We might be young, but we were tough. And we had the buggy. True, we'd never made a trip across, and the truck was only now in working order. But we were gearing up for it. We wanted to join Uncle Joe in the business of transporting outlaws across the valley to Hider's Haven.

He was the only one in the whole town brave enough to make the trip, but he was getting old and we wanted to take over for him. The pay was good. Even better, I wouldn't have to let anyone pinch me on the butt.

There weren't a lot of jobs for girls on the run. We could only be paid under the table, which made it hard.

"Even if he was wounded, Uncle Joe would find a way to activate the charm," Bree said.

As if he'd heard her, the charm around Bree's neck lit up, golden and bright.

She looked down, eyes widening. "Holy fates."

Panic sliced through me. My gaze met hers, then darted to Rowan's. Worry glinted in both their eyes.

"We have to go," Rowan said.

I nodded, my mind racing. This was *real*. We'd only ever

talked about crossing the valley. Planned and planned and planned.

But this was *go time*.

"Is the buggy ready?" I asked.

"As ready as it'll ever be," Rowan said.

My gaze traced over it. The truck was a hulking beast, with huge, sturdy tires and platforms built over the front hood and the back. We'd only ever heard stories of the monsters out in Death Valley, but we needed a place from which to fight them and the platforms should do the job. The huge spikes on the sides would help, but we'd be responsible for fending off most of the monsters.

All of the cars in Death Valley Junction looked like something out of *Mad Max*, but ours was one of the few that had been built to cross the valley.

At least, we hoped it could cross.

We had some magic to help us out, at least. I could create shields, Bree could shoot sonic booms, and Rowan could move things with her mind.

Rowan's gaze drifted to the sun that was high in the sky. "Not the best time to go, but I don't see how we have a choice."

I nodded. No one wanted to cross the valley in the day. According to Uncle Joe, it was the most dangerous of all. But things must be really bad if he'd pressed the button now.

He was probably hoping we were smart enough to wait to cross.

We weren't.

"Let's get dressed and go." I hurried up the creaky front steps and into the ramshackle house.

It didn't take long to dig through my meager possessions and find the leather pants and strappy top that would be my fight wear for out in the valley. It was too hot for anything more, though night would bring the cold.

Daggers were my preferred weapon—mostly since they were cheaper than swords and I had good aim with anything small and pointy. I shoved as many as I could into the little pockets built into the outside of my boots and pants. A small duffel full of daggers completed my arsenal.

I grabbed a leather jacket and the sand goggles that I'd gotten second hand, then ran out of the room. I nearly collided with Bree, whose blue eyes were bright with worry.

"We can do this," I said.

She nodded. "You're right. It's been our plan all along."

I swallowed hard, mind racing with all the things that could go wrong. The valley was full of monsters and dangerous challenges—and according to Uncle Joe, they changed every day. We had no idea what would be coming at us, but we couldn't turn back.

Not with Uncle Joe on the other side.

We swung by the kitchen to grab jugs of water and some food, then hurried out of the house. Rowan was already in the driver's seat, ready to go. Her sand goggles were pushed up on her head, and her leather top looked like armor.

"Get a move on!" she shouted.

I raced to the truck and scrambled up onto the back platform. Though I could open the side door, I was still wary of the Ravener poison Rowan had painted onto the spikes. It would paralyze me for twenty-four hours, and that was the last thing we needed.

Bree scrambled up to join me, and we tossed the supplies onto the floorboard of the back seat, then joined Rowan in the front, sitting on the long bench.

She cranked the engine, which grumbled and roared, then pulled away from the house.

"Holy crap, it's happening." Excitement and fear shivered across my skin.

Worry was a familiar foe. I'd been worried my whole life. Worried about hiding from the unknown people who hunted us. Worried about paying the bills. Worried about my sisters. But it'd never done me any good. So I shoved aside my fear for Uncle Joe and focused on what was ahead.

The wind tore through my hair as Rowan drove away from Death Valley Junction, cutting across the desert floor as the sun blazed down. I shielded my eyes, scouting the mountains ahead. The range rose tall, cast in shadows of gray and beige.

Bree pointed to a path that had been worn through the scrubby ground. "Try here!"

Rowan turned right, and the buggy cut toward the mountains. There was a parallel valley—the *real* Death Valley— that only supernaturals could access. That was what we had to cross.

Rowan drove straight for one of the shallower inclines, slowing the buggy as it climbed up the mountain. The big tires dug into the ground, and I prayed they'd hold up. We'd built most of the buggy from secondhand stuff, and there was no telling what was going to give out first.

The three of us leaned forward as we neared the top, and I swore I could hear our heartbeats pounding in unison. When we crested the ridge and spotted the valley spread out below us, my breath caught.

It was beautiful. And terrifying. The long valley had to be at least a hundred miles long and several miles wide. Different colors swirled across the ground, looking like they simmered with heat.

Danger cloaked the place, dark magic that made my skin crawl.

"Welcome to hell," Bree muttered.

"I kinda like it," I said. "It's terrifying but..."

"Awesome," Rowan said.

"You are both nuts," Bree said. "Now drive us down there. I'm ready to fight some monsters."

Rowan saluted and pulled the buggy over the mountain ridge, then navigated her way down the mountainside.

"I wonder what will hit us first?" My heart raced at the thought.

"Could be anything," Bree said. "Bad Water has monsters, kaleidoscope dunes has all kinds of crazy shit, and the arches could be trouble."

We were at least a hundred miles from Hider's Haven, though Uncle Joe said the distances could change sometimes. Anything could come at us in that amount of time.

Rowan pulled the buggy onto the flat ground.

"I'll take the back." I undid my seatbelt and scrambled up onto the back platform.

Bree climbed onto the front platform, carrying her sword.

"Hang on tight!" Rowan cried.

I gripped the safety railing that we'd installed on the back platform and crouched to keep my balance. She hit the gas, and the buggy jumped forward.

Rowan laughed like a loon and drove us straight into hell.

Up ahead, the ground shimmered in the sun, glowing silver.

"What do you think that is?" Rowan called.

"I don't know," I shouted. "Go around!"

She turned left, trying to cut around the reflective ground, but the silver just extended into our path, growing wider and wider. Death Valley moving to accommodate us.

Moving to trap us.

Then the silver raced toward us, stretching across the ground.

There was no way around.

"You're going to have to drive over it!" I shouted.

She hit the gas harder, and the buggy sped up. The reflective surface glinted in the sun, and as the tires passed over it, water kicked up from the wheels.

"It's the Bad Water!" I cried.

The old salt lake was sometimes dried up, sometimes not. But it wasn't supposed to be deep. Six inches, max. Right?

Please be right, Uncle Joe.

Rowan sped over the water, the buggy's tires sending up silver spray that sparkled in the sunlight. It smelled like rotten eggs, and I gagged, then breathed shallowly through my mouth.

Magic always had a signature—taste, smell, sound. Something that lit up one of the five senses. Maybe more.

And a rotten egg stink was bad news. That meant dark magic.

Tension fizzed across my skin as we drove through the Bad Water. On either side of the car, water sprayed up from the wheels in a dazzling display that belied the danger of the situation. By the time the explosion came, I was strung so tight that I almost leapt off the platform.

The monster was as wide as the buggy, but so long that I couldn't see where it began or ended. It was a massive sea creature with fangs as long as my arm and brilliant blue eyes. Silver scales were the same color as the water, which was still only six inches deep, thank fates.

Magic propelled the monster, who circled our vehicle, his body glinting in the sun. He had to be a hundred feet long, with black wings and claws. He climbed on the ground and leapt into the air, slithering around as he examined us.

"It's the Unhcegila!" Bree cried from the front.

Shit.

Uncle Joe had told us about the Unhcegila—a terrifying water monster from Dakota and Lakota Sioux legends.

Except it was real, as all good legends were. And it occasionally appeared when the Bad Water wasn't dried up. It only needed a few inches to appear.

Looked like it was our lucky day.

~~~

Join my mailing list at www.linseyhall.com/subscribe to continue the adventure and get a free ebook copy of *Death Valley Magic*. No spam and you can leave anytime!

AUTHOR'S NOTE

Thank you for reading *Power of Magic!* As with my other books, I like to include historical places and mythological elements.

Rowan's series has been super fun to write because we know so much about the ancient Greeks and their religion. Many of those elements were as I presented them in the story, but some were modified.

One of the modifications in this book were the Echidna. According to written record, there was only one Echidna, and she was called the Mother of Monsters. Her famous offspring (with Typhon, the most fearsome monster in all of Greek myth) include Cerberus, the Sphinx, the Chimera, and the Lernaean Hydra. I chose to have three Echidna in Rowan's story simply because it's fun.

You may have recognized Medusa from one of my other books. She was only briefly mentioned in Nix's series, but she had the same origin story in that book as well. Nix identified that Medusa wasn't actually an evil character, but the story didn't take her as far as rescuing her. However, the treatment of Medusa in Greek myth has always bothered me, so I thought it would be a good for Rowan to tackle the issue.

As I mention in the book, there are multiple origin stories for Medusa. One of the most famous ones is Ovid's, in which Medusa is raped by Poseidon and then punished by Athena, who gives her the snake hair and ability to turn men to stone. Where's the logic in that? Honestly, it just sucks. To make matters worse, the famous greek hero Perseus made it clear in Ovid's tale that he thought Medusa deserved her fate. He then killed her in order to complete the tasks given to him by King Polydectes. Doesn't sound like a hero to me. Since I loathe how Medusa was treated, one of the highlights of the book for me was getting to write Rowan as a true hero who saves her.

In fact, one of my favorite elements of Rowan's story is that she rescues the women who were wronged by the gods. First Daphne and Lotus, who were trapped in trees to "save" them from lusty (rapey) gods, and then Medusa. Even Arachne, who chose to stay in her spider form, was given the option of help. I'm sure that if I did a little more research, I could find plenty more women (and a few men, too) that Rowan could rescue.

That's not to say all of the gods were bad—they are fascinating and cool in many ways. I've really enjoyed writing them. But there are some elements that I was happy to rewrite in Rowan's story.

I think that's it for the history and mythology in *Power of Magic*—at least the big things. I hope you enjoyed the book and will come back for more of the FireSouls and Dragon Gods's worlds.

To Carey, with love.

ACKNOWLEDGMENTS

Thank you, Ben, for everything. There would be no books without you.

Thank you to Jena O'Connor and Lindsey Loucks for your excellent editing. The book is immensely better because of you!

Thank you to Orina Kafe for the beautiful cover art. Thank you to Collette Markwardt for allowing me to borrow the Pugs of Destruction, who are real dogs named Chaos, Havoc, and Ruckus. They were all adopted from rescue agencies.

ABOUT LINSEY

Before becoming a writer, Linsey Hall was a nautical archaeologist who studied shipwrecks from Hawaii and the Yukon to the UK and the Mediterranean. She credits fantasy and historical romances with her love of history and her career as an archaeologist. After a decade of tromping around the globe in search of old bits of stuff that people left lying about, she settled down and started penning her own romance novels. Her Dragon's Gift series draws upon her love of history and the paranormal elements that she can't help but include.

COPYRIGHT

52290309R00133

Made in the USA
Columbia, SC
01 March 2019